Enrollment Form

☐ *Yes!* I WANT TO BE A *Privileged Woman*.
Enclosed is one *PAGES & PRIVILEGES™* Proof of Purchase from any Harlequin or Silhouette book currently for sale in stores (Proofs of Purchase are found on the back pages of books) and the store cash register receipt. Please enroll me in *PAGES & PRIVILEGES™*. Send my Welcome Kit and FREE Gifts — and activate my FREE benefits — immediately.

More great gifts and benefits to come.

NAME (please print)
_____

ADDRESS _____ APT. NO _____

CITY _____ STATE _____ ZIP/POSTAL CODE _____

PROOF OF PURCHASE ONLY

NO CLUB!
NO COMMITMENT!
Just one purchase brings you great Free Gifts and Benefits!

Please allow 6-8 weeks for delivery. Quantities are limited. We reserve the right to substitute items. Enroll before October 31, 1995 and receive one full year of benefits.

Name of store where this book was purchased_____

Date of purchase_____

Type of store:
☐ Bookstore   ☐ Supermarket   ☐ Drugstore
☐ Dept. or discount store (e.g. K-Mart or Walmart)
☐ Other (specify)_____

Which Harlequin or Silhouette series do you usually read?
_____

Complete and mail with one Proof of Purchase and store receipt to:
U.S.: *PAGES & PRIVILEGES™*, P.O. Box 1960, Danbury, CT 06813-1960
Canada: *PAGES & PRIVILEGES™*, 49-6A The Donway West, P.O. 813, North York, ON M3C 2E8

SSE-PP6B

▼ DETACH HERE AND MAIL TODAY! ▼

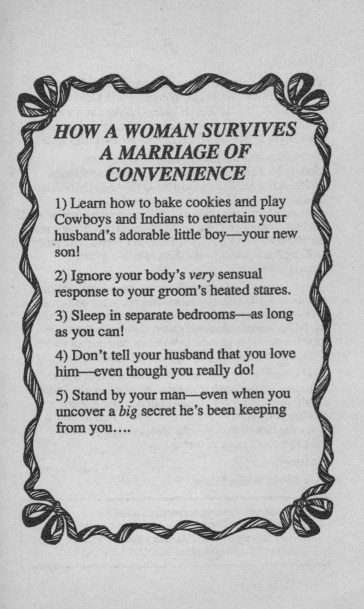

HOW A WOMAN SURVIVES A MARRIAGE OF CONVENIENCE

1) Learn how to bake cookies and play Cowboys and Indians to entertain your husband's adorable little boy—your new son!

2) Ignore your body's *very* sensual response to your groom's heated stares.

3) Sleep in separate bedrooms—as long as you can!

4) Don't tell your husband that you love him—even though you really do!

5) Stand by your man—even when you uncover a *big* secret he's been keeping from you....

Dear Reader,

There's a lot in store for you this month from Silhouette Special Edition! We begin, of course, with October's THAT SPECIAL WOMAN! title, *D Is for Dani's Baby*, by Lisa Jackson. It's another heartwarming and emotional installment in her LOVE LETTERS series. Don't miss it!

We haven't seen the last of Morgan Trayhern as Lindsay McKenna returns with a marvelous new series, MORGAN'S MERCENARIES: LOVE AND DANGER. You'll want to be there for every spine-tingling and passionately romantic tale, and it all starts with *Morgan's Wife*. And for those of you who have been eagerly following the delightful ALWAYS A BRIDESMAID! series, look no further, as Katie Jones is able to say she's *Finally a Bride*, by Sherryl Woods.

Also this month, it's city girl versus roguish rancher in *A Man and a Million*, by Jackie Merritt. A second chance at love—and a secret long kept—awaits in *This Child Is Mine*, by Trisha Alexander. And finally, October is Premiere month, and we're pleased to welcome new author Laurie Campbell and her story *And Father Makes Three*.

Next month we're beginning our celebration of Special Edition's 1000th book with some of your favorite authors! Don't miss books from Diana Palmer, Nora Roberts and Debbie Macomber—just to name a few! I know you'll enjoy the blockbuster months ahead. I hope you enjoy each and every story to come!

Sincerely,

Tara Gavin, Senior Editor

Please address questions and book requests to:
Silhouette Reader Service
U.S.: 3010 Walden Ave., P.O. Box 1325, Buffalo, NY 14269
Canadian: P.O. Box 609, Fort Erie, Ont. L2A 5X3

Sherryl Woods
Finally A Bride

Silhouette®

SPECIAL EDITION®

Published by Silhouette Books

America's Publisher of Contemporary Romance

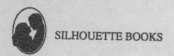

SILHOUETTE BOOKS

ISBN 0-373-09987-8

FINALLY A BRIDE

Books by Sherryl Woods

Silhouette Special Edition

Safe Harbor #425
Never Let Go #446
Edge of Forever #484
In Too Deep #522
Miss Liz's Passion #573
Tea and Destiny #595
My Dearest Cal #669
Joshua and the Cowgirl #713
*Love #769
*Honor #775
*Cherish #781
*Kate's Vow #823
*A Daring Vow #855
*A Vow to Love #885
The Parson's Waiting #907
One Step Away #927
Riley's Sleeping Beauty #961
‡Finally a Bride #987

*Vows
‡Always a Bridesmaid!

Silhouette Desire

Not at Eight, Darling #309
Yesterday's Love #329
Come Fly with Me #345
A Gift of Love #375
Can't Say No #431
Heartland #472
One Touch of Moondust #521
Next Time...Forever #601
Fever Pitch #620
Dream Mender #708

Silhouette Books

Silhouette Summer Sizzlers
1990 "A Bridge to Dreams"

SHERRYL WOODS

lives by the ocean, which, she says, provides daily inspiration for the romance in her soul. She further explains that her years as a television critic taught her about steamy plots and humor; her years as a travel editor took her to exotic locations; and her years as a crummy weekend tennis player taught her to stick with what she enjoyed most—writing. "What better way is there," Sherryl asks, "to combine all that experience than by creating romantic stories?" Sherryl loves to hear from her readers. You may write to her at P.O. Box 490326, Key Biscayne, FL 33149. A self-addressed stamped envelope is appreciated for a reply.

CAST OF CHARACTERS

The Women:

Hannah Farley: Blue-blooded bad girl.

Emma Wynn: Once burned, twice shy.

Sophie Reynolds: Single mom with secrets.

Lucy Maguire: Not left at the altar for long.

Katie Jones: Always a bridesmaid…

The Men:

Matthew Granger: Stranger in a small town.

Michael Flint: Mr. Wrong has never been so right.

Ford Maguire: Lucy's lawman brother falls for
                  shady lady?

Max Ryder: Mystery man appears in the nick of
                  time.

Luke Cassidy: Single dad makes impassioned plea.

The woman who's always a bridesmaid is finally a bride! She's getting a handsome groom, gaining an adorable son and marrying the man she's always loved. Problem is, her marriage to Luke Cassidy will be in name only! And has Luke told Katie the real reason he needs a wife by tomorrow?

Find out as Always a Bridesmaid! concludes this month. (You won't want to miss the big wedding!)

Prologue

"You're going to need a new roof," Ron Matthews informed Caitlyn Jones, gesturing toward the upper levels of the Clover Street Boarding House. "If you don't replace the whole thing, you'll just have me up there patching after every single thunderstorm rolls through here all summer long, and you'll still need a new roof when all's said and done."

Katie heard the news with a sinking sensation in the pit of her stomach. First the wiring, then the plumbing, now the roof. Was there any part of this beautiful old Victorian house that wasn't about to collapse around her?

The repairs were sopping up the last of her savings at a rate that made her banker very nervous. Charlie Hastings at the First National Bank of Clover, South

Carolina, had already started asking pointed questions about where she was going to find the funds to make the balloon payment on her mortgage on the first of September. He was all too aware of the state of her bank balance and her pitiful cash flow.

He also knew in intimate detail what she'd already spent to make the once decrepit boarding house habitable after years of neglect. And he was just itching to remind her he'd warned her about all the pitfalls of taking an old relic and trying to remodel it on a shoestring budget. In essence, Charlie Hastings was a royal pain. Just the thought of admitting to him that he'd been right had her sighing heavily.

''Trouble?''

Katie's heart thumped unsteadily at the sound of that one single word. She recognized Luke Cassidy's voice as if she'd last heard it only yesterday. Instead it had been six years ago, on a night filled with the kind of seductive whispers that had made her heart melt. *Trouble?* Luke Cassidy's return to Clover made the problems with the boarding house pale in comparison.

She'd been dreading a face-to-face meeting with Luke ever since he'd hit town. She'd hoped it would come when she was dressed fit to kill, rather than wearing ragged cutoffs and a cast-off man's shirt that had belonged to one of her elderly boarders.

''Nothing I can't handle,'' she insisted, turning slowly toward the man who had broken her heart by abandoning her without a word of goodbye.

Aware that news of this meeting would spread through town like lightning, she faced him squarely.

She raised her chin a notch just to show that his disappearance had meant nothing to her, that *he* meant nothing to her, despite all the years of friendship that had preceded that one stolen night of perfect bliss.

To prove just how independent she'd become and how unflustered she was by Luke's presence, she shifted her gaze to Ron. "How soon can you start working on the roof?"

"What will it cost?" Luke asked, avoiding her entirely and concentrating on the roofer who'd been one class behind Katie in school.

Ron's gaze darted from Katie to Luke and back again. Apparently he caught something in her expression that made him ignore Luke and respond directly to her.

"Week after next is the soonest, Katie," he said apologetically. "I'll put a tarp over it meantime. That should keep the worst of any rain from leaking into that front bedroom until I can get to it."

"Thanks, Ron."

"How much?" Luke repeated as if he had a perfect right to ask the question.

Ron regarded him doubtfully, then looked at Katie. She sighed. "How much?" she repeated.

"Four thousand. Could be closer to five with all those turrets. It's not like slapping up a nice straight roof on some little single-story bungalow. I'll get you a firm estimate by tomorrow."

Katie gulped. *Four or five thousand dollars!* Where was she supposed to come up with that kind of money? Right now, though, it hardly mattered. She wouldn't back down from the commitment with Luke looking on if her life depended on it.

"Fine," she said, though there was the faintest tremor in her voice she couldn't control.

"Is that a problem?" Ron asked, picking up on that tremor. "If it is, all you have to do is say the word and we can work out the payments. You know I'd do anything in the world to help you make a go of this place, Katie."

"I'll manage," Katie snapped, then winced at her misdirected anger. If anyone deserved sharp words it was Luke, not Ron, and it was way too late to be delivering them. "Just schedule the job, Ron. I had to move Mrs. Jeffers into another room until the repairs are done. I can't afford to keep a room empty for long."

"Sure thing. If I can free up someone to start sooner, I'll let you know." He glanced at Luke. "Good to see you again, Luke. I'd heard you were back. Planning to stay?"

Luke nodded. "If things work out," he said enigmatically.

As soon as the roofer had left, Kate whirled on Luke. "How dare you interfere in this? The cost of repairing my roof is none of your business."

"Never said it was," he said complacently, shoving his hands into the pockets of his worn jeans. "But you weren't asking and the question needed answering. Spelling out the details is one of the cardinal rules in business. Getting it in writing is another."

The suggestion that she had been about to make a lousy business decision and didn't know enough to get a contract aggravated Katie almost as much as Luke's interference.

"Ron and I have done a lot of business together," she said.

His knowing glance took in the old Victorian from porch to roof. "I can imagine."

His sarcasm had her gnashing her teeth. "We would have discussed the cost."

"When?"

"Later." She scowled at him, hoping her frosty reception would drive him away before she betrayed the fact that his presence had her heart hammering a hundred beats a minute. "Did you want something in particular?"

"You and Ron seem...close," he said, watching her intently. "How close?"

"Oh, I'm sure if you hadn't been here, he would have thrown me to the lawn and made mad, passionate love to me," she said sweetly.

Luke's jaw clenched. "That's not something to joke about."

"It's also none of your business."

"So you've said. Well, let's just pretend for a moment that it is my business. How close are you?"

"Oh, for pity's sake, Luke, Ron is happily married and has three kids."

"Then how come he's so eager to give you a break on the roof job?"

If Luke hadn't looked so genuinely bemused by Ron's generosity, Katie might have blown a gasket at the suggestion that the younger man might expect something in return. As it was, she figured it was about time Luke learned that not every relationship was about sex. Maybe, after all those years of well-reported wheeling and dealing in Atlanta, he needed to remember that in Clover people helped each other out without ulterior motives.

"Ron's kid sister was one of my first boarders," she said. "She was having a rough time at home. When she moved in here, I looked out for her. He credits me with keeping her out of trouble, though the truth is Janie was smarter than anyone in her family recognized. She had her whole life mapped out, and it didn't include getting smashed up with a bunch of teenage drunks out on the highway or an unplanned pregnancy. More kids today should have the kinds of goals and limits she'd set for herself."

If she hadn't had her gaze pinned to Luke's face, Katie might have missed the fleeting change in his expression when she mentioned the unplanned pregnancy. It made her wonder all over again how much the son he'd turned up with on his return had to do with his abrupt departure all those years ago. Just guessing that the timing roughly coincided with the same period in which he'd made love to her filled her with regrets. If Luke had been trapped into marriage, why couldn't she have been the one...? She let the thought trail off uncompleted. She would never have done that to him. Never.

Whatever Luke was thinking, though, he managed to banish it. He resumed that bland, inscrutable expression that tempted Katie to do something, *anything* to draw a reaction.

Regarding her evenly, he asked, "How are you going to pay for a new roof?"

The question was so far afield from the direction of her thoughts that Katie took a minute to form a response. "That's what you dropped by after six years to ask?"

Luke's mouth tightened into a grim line. "How are you going to pay for it?"

"I'll find a way," she said, injecting a misplaced note of confidence into her voice. "Well, it was great seeing you again. We'll have to catch up some other time. I've got things to do."

She tried to subtly edge toward the front door, but Luke kept pace with her. She sighed at her failed attempt to escape. He'd always had a single-track mind and an inability to take a hint.

"How? By working more hours at Peg's Diner?" he asked irritably. "You can't earn enough there in the next week to pay for the tarp Ron is going to use, much less a new roof."

She stared at him, filled with indignation at the certainty she heard in his voice. "How would you know a thing like that? And what difference does it make to you, even if it is true?"

"It's not all that difficult to get information in Clover," he said. "Nothing thrives in this town quite like gossip."

"You used to hate that," Katie reminded him.

"Yes, I did," he agreed. "I've discovered, though, that it has its uses. The rumor mill provided all the information I needed on you, including the fact that you are knee-deep in debt. Half the people I talked to are worried sick about you. They say you're wearing yourself out trying to make a go of this business. What in all that's holy ever possessed you to buy this ramshackle old place and try to turn it into a boarding house? It should have been torn down thirty years ago when the McAllisters abandoned it.''

I bought it because we used to sit on that secluded porch night after night and share our innermost secrets, she thought to herself. Those were memories he'd obviously forgotten. She wouldn't have divulged them to him now for a stack of free shingles and sufficient tar paper to cover the entire roof. She decided it was best to ignore that question altogether.

''I had no idea folks in Clover were so fascinated with my well-being.'' She regarded him pointedly. ''But they, at least, are friends. I'm not sure I'd describe you the same way. I do know that my financial status is none of your concern. I can't imagine why you would have wanted information about me, but if you did, you could have asked me directly.''

''Would you have given me honest answers?''

Their gazes clashed. ''I was always honest with you,'' she said heatedly. ''You...'' She let the accusation trail off. There was no point to arguing. History couldn't be changed. She had loved him once to distraction. He had left her without a word, apparently to marry a woman who was pregnant with his child. What more was there to say?

Even though Katie fell silent, Luke clearly got the message and, just as clearly, accepted the blame for whatever lack of honesty had come between them six years earlier. Guilt was written all over his handsome, chiseled face, along with something that might have been regret.

"Look, can we go inside and talk?" he asked, his tone suddenly placating.

"Why?"

He seemed amused by her reluctance. "Maybe just because it's way past time for two old friends to catch up."

Catching up—risking involvement—struck Katie as a remarkably bad idea. She didn't want to be alone with Luke. The man still had the power to wreak havoc with her senses. She'd known that the instant she'd spotted him in the back of the church at Lucy Maguire Ryder's disrupted wedding. That meant he also had the power to cause her even more anguish than he had in the past. She had wounds from the first time that, to her deep regret, felt as fresh today as they had on the day he'd walked out of her life.

"Please," he coaxed, his gaze unrelenting.

"We can sit on the porch," she said as a compromise when she saw that he wasn't about to leave until he'd gotten whatever he'd come for. She didn't for one single minute believe it had anything to do with the cost of her roof repairs. "I'll get us some lemonade."

"Afraid to be alone with me?" he inquired with a smile that never quite reached his eyes.

"Never," she denied.

"Then wouldn't it be better to have this conversation where half the town won't be witness to it?"

She couldn't imagine what he had to say that needed such privacy, but it was clear he was going to badger her until he got his way. "Oh, for heaven's sakes," she snapped impatiently. "Come on into the kitchen."

The kitchen, normally Katie's favorite room in the house because of its huge windows facing the backyard and a table large enough to seat a half-dozen friends for a good long chat, suddenly seemed the size of a closet. Luke's presence was overpowering. The effect was worsened by his pacing, which brought him brushing past her time and again as she squeezed the lemons into a big glass pitcher, added water, plenty of sugar and a tray of ice cubes. At least the process and his silence gave her time to gather her composure.

When she finally turned, handing him a glass, she was almost able to convince herself that Luke was just another old friend stopping by to catch up on the news. People—a few of them attractive, available men—gathered in her kitchen all the time, though none of them made her pulse race. Still, there was no reason to think of Luke any differently than she did all those others. She could handle his presence. She could, dammit!

Then his fingers grazed hers as he took the lemonade. Her pulse bucked. She glanced into his eyes and saw a torment that made her breath catch in her throat. Her natural compassion welled up, even as she forced herself to look away. It took every ounce of restraint she possessed to keep from wrapping her arms around him and consoling him.

Though what Luke Cassidy had to be tormented about she couldn't imagine. Everyone in town had heard by now that he'd made a fortune while living in Atlanta. He had a precious son, Robby, the merest sight of whom brought a lump to Katie's throat. And if he was divorced, well, so were a lot of people. However tragic the circumstances, people got over it. It was nothing for her to get all teary-eyed over.

"Katie?" Luke asked suddenly.

She reluctantly lifted her gaze to his. Something in his voice, a soft, cajoling note, made her pulse skip yet another beat. How many times had she heard just that note before he'd asked her to do something outrageous? She could tell by the gleam in his eyes that he intended to do just that all over again.

"What?" she asked warily.

"Marry me."

The two simple, totally unexpected words hit her with the force of a tornado. If he'd asked her to join him on a shuttle to the moon, she wouldn't have been any more stunned. Katie was suddenly very glad they weren't in plain sight. At least there was no one to see her mouth drop open, no one to witness in case she followed through on her urge to whap him upside his hard head with a frying pan. If Luke Cassidy had asked her to marry him six years ago, she would have wept with joy. Today that same request—that out-of-the-blue mockery of a real proposal—filled her with fury.

"You want to marry me?" she repeated incredulously. Her pulse, apparently unaware that the proposal merited anger, not consideration, took off as if this were a declaration of true love. "Six years without a word, and now you want to marry me? Just like that?"

"Just like that," he agreed, as calmly as if the suggestion weren't totally absurd.

"Have you lost your mind?"

He seemed to consider the question thoughtfully, then shook his head, his expression thoroughly serious. "Nope. I don't think so."

"Then I think you need a second opinion."

"Katie, I've given this a lot of thought. It makes sense."

She regarded him blankly. "Why?" she asked, when she should have been shrieking to the high heavens about the gall of any man who would walk back into a woman's life after six years and drop a marriage proposal on the table as if it were a simple hello.

"Why?" she asked again, wondering if there was a snowball's chance in hell that she would get the simple, three-word answer she'd always dreamed of hearing cross his lips.

"My son needs a mother. You need somebody to put this place on a sound financial base again. We always got along. I think we could make it work."

Not three words, but a litany, Katie noticed in disgust as Luke ticked off the reasons matter-of-factly. He'd probably made a damn list of them. His businesslike tone made her grind her teeth.

"You sound as if you're negotiating for the merger of two companies with compatible products," she accused.

The idiot didn't even have the decency to deny it.

"That's one way of looking at it, I suppose," he agreed, looking pleased that she had grasped the concept. "We both get something we need. I knew I could count on you not to get all sloppy and sentimental about this."

Katie was just itching to reach for the cast iron skillet that was sitting atop her twenty-year-old stove, when she made the mistake of looking again into Luke's eyes for a second time. Those blue eyes that had once danced with laughter were flat and empty now. Lonely. Lost.

Katie had always been a sucker for a lost soul. And from her twelfth birthday, when he'd brought her a wilted, but flamboyantly huge bouquet of wildflowers, she had been a sucker for Luke Cassidy. Regrettably, nothing in the past six years they'd been apart had changed that.

She drew in a deep, steadying breath and realized that she was going to do it. She was going to say yes and damn the consequences.

"Oh, what the hell," she murmured, furious with herself for not having the willpower to resist this man or the son he'd just turned up with. Maybe she'd just been a spinster too darn long. More likely, she'd just missed Luke too much, something she wouldn't tell him if he hog-tied her and dragged her through town in full view of every single person who'd watched the two of them grow up. Cursing herself for being a pathetic, love-starved wimp, she tried valiantly to list all the reasons to say an emphatic no. There were dozens of them, but she couldn't seem to force her lips to form the first one.

At her continued silence, a faint suggestion of a grin tugged at Luke's mouth. "Was that a yes?"

It was and they both knew it, but she wouldn't make it easy on him. Katie knew she didn't have Luke's business acumen, but she did have an instinct for self-preservation. She couldn't just cave in and accept his first offer. If he wanted a coldhearted business deal, then that's what he'd get.

"We need to discuss terms," she said, keeping her voice as matter-of-fact as his, even though her heart was thundering wildly.

She couldn't believe what she was about to do. She was standing in her own kitchen, negotiating with a man she'd loved forever, about a blasted marriage of convenience. She ought to have her head examined. She was apparently every bit as loony as he was.

Then again, as everyone who knew her well would understand, her head had never had much to do with her feelings for Luke. It was her heart he had stolen and apparently intended to claim now as his own.

Still, there was a definite call for putting some emotional distance between them, for hanging on to a shred of dignity. She would not rush into his arms, allowing herself to think for one single instant that he actually cared a whit for her. He wanted a mother for his child. She would be a baby-sitter with unusual benefits. That was it. She supposed people had gotten married for less rational reasons, but she'd never met any of them.

A few centuries back marriages like this had even been arranged by doting, practical fathers. She'd always considered such arrangements barbaric. Now she found herself in the unique position of working out such terms for herself. Well, Luke could be darned sure that she was going to adequately protect herself from any more of his foolish whims.

She went to the kitchen counter, picked up a pad of paper and a pen, then sat down at the table, pen poised. "I'm ready. Let's talk."

"Okay," he said, suddenly cautious. "What did you have in mind?"

"A contract with everything all spelled out on paper. Didn't you remind me just a few minutes ago that that's how business is done?" she asked sweetly.

"Katie," he began in a warning tone.

She ignored the warning. "This is my boarding house. I run it as I see fit." She jotted that down before he could say a word.

"Now, wait a minute," he protested. "Running it how you see fit is what got you into this mess."

She looked him straight in the eye. "I run it. I deal with the guests," she insisted. "You can handle the business end of things, if you want."

"Thank you so much," he said.

She frowned at his mocking tone. "This won't work, if you're going to be surly."

"I am never surly."

Katie rolled her eyes. "You haven't changed that much, Luke Cassidy. You were always surly, especially when you weren't getting your way."

She studied him consideringly. He wasn't exactly dressed for success today, but she wasn't fooled by the faded, skintight jeans, the rumpled yellow shirt or the battered sneakers. She knew the kind of money the man had made. She'd saved every one of the clippings from the local paper enumerating his financial achievements. Luke might not have been back in Clover for years, but his press releases had been.

"I'd say an investment in the Clover Street Boarding House would be appropriate, wouldn't you? Say ten thousand," she said and wrote it down. "That will take care of the roof and a few odds and ends I haven't been able to afford, plus some of that balloon payment that's due in September."

"You want ten thousand dollars in return for agreeing to marry me?" he repeated, his neck turning a dull red. "Selling yourself cheap, aren't you?"

She nodded as the shot hit its mark and crossed off what she'd written. "You have a point. Make that ten thousand a year for the first five years. Guaranteed," she added, "even if the marriage falls apart."

This time, he was the one who looked as if she'd tried to flatten him with a two-by-four. Katie was rather pleased with herself.

"You can't be serious," he said.

"Oh, but I am. Putting this place on a sound financial base is what this deal is all about, right? From my point of view, that is."

She beamed at him. "Now, then, as far as me being a mother to Robby, we make decisions about him together. You don't just start bullying me around or pull rank whenever I do something that doesn't suit you. A child's parents should present a united front. Squabbling will just confuse him."

"What the hell do you know about raising a child?"

"I've watched all those baby doctors on TV. Besides, you're the one who picked me to be a mother to your son. Are you changing your mind?"

Based on Luke's stunned expression, Katie had the feeling she'd finally turned this stupid game of his to her advantage. The fact that he hadn't stormed out the door was a testament to how committed he was to this plan he'd dreamed up.

"Okay," he said, his teeth clenched. "You win."

"Good." She nodded approvingly as she made a note. "Just one last thing."

"Only one more?"

Katie glared at him. "We have separate bedrooms. You can have the one that's empty right now, as soon as the roof's repaired, of course. I wouldn't expect you to sleep in it while the rain is pouring in. And we want to give Robby a few weeks to get to know me before we set the date."

"Now wait just a minute," he protested. "What the hell kind of marriage is that? Husbands and wives do not sleep in separate bedrooms."

"That's true enough for ordinary husbands and wives." She shrugged. "You're the one who established this as some sort of business arrangement. I have no idea what your code of ethics is like after all this time, but I don't sleep with business partners. I wouldn't think you'd want any messy emotional entanglements, either. Sex has a way of muddying things up."

"How would you know?" he muttered, scowling at her.

She could tell that she had taken him by surprise with her list of demands, especially this last one. She couldn't imagine what Luke had been thinking by making this ridiculous proposition to her this morning. But if he had expected her to fall into bed with a man who could suggest this cold, calculated arrangement, then he was sadly mistaken.

She might love him to distraction, but she would never let him see her vulnerability. She knew that if Luke so much as touched her, she would go up in flames. It had always been that way. She doubted that time had dulled the effect. Time obviously hadn't done a thing to correct her inability to think straight around him. Just look at the crazy agreement she was about to enter into. She suspected it was like making a bargain with the devil. No matter how many concessions a person gained, there was no way to win in the long run. But she intended to give Luke Cassidy a run for his money.

"Those are my terms," she repeated, meeting his gaze evenly. She held out the tablet on which she'd written every last detail of their agreement. "Sign it."

He seemed a little bewildered by her stance, but he nodded finally, scrawled his name across the bottom, then held out his hand. "It looks like we have a deal."

"So it does," she said, avoiding his hand as if it were contaminated. One touch, she reminded herself. Just one and this cool attitude of hers would be ashes.

"I'll be in touch to work out the wedding plans," Luke said, sounding satisfied—or relieved?—now that the deal was concluded.

As he left, Katie clutched the signed contract and fought to contain a sigh of regret. So much for moonlight and roses and a proposal that came from the heart. That was just one more silly yearning she would have to pack away. After being a bridesmaid more times than she could recall for Hannah, Emma and all the others, she would finally have her wedding. She'd finally have the only man she'd ever loved.

But it would all be a sham.

Chapter One

The upcoming wedding of Caitlyn Jones and Luke Cassidy was the hottest topic at the Clover Beauty Boutique on the first Monday morning in June when Lucy Maguire Ryder, just back from her own honeymoon, divulged the news. When she discovered she'd scooped the bride and groom, Lucy rushed to Peg's Diner to apologize.

Naturally Lucy's apology and the reason for it were overheard and within seconds the news had spread from one end of the diner to the other. Katie could barely squeeze through the center aisle to deliver the rush of morning orders of eggs and grits for all the well-wishers stopping her to offer congratulations and best wishes. Periodically, as she poured cups of her

Aunt Peg's potent special blend coffee, she paused long enough to glare at Lucy.

"I'm sorry," Lucy said again when Katie was finally able to take a break. "I thought for sure you would have told everyone by now. The wedding's this Saturday, for heaven's sakes."

"You sound just like Luke. He's getting impatient, too."

"Well, I can't say that I blame him. You're acting as if this is something you're ashamed of. What does Peg say about it? Is she thrilled about the wedding?"

Katie winced as guilt sliced through her. "I haven't told her yet. Thank goodness she's off this morning. If she found out like this she'd never forgive me. And I'd have you to blame for spilling the beans."

Lucy was clearly aghast. "Katie, at this rate you would have been celebrating your tenth anniversary before anyone was the wiser. People were bound to wonder why you kept the news secret. I know there are . . ."

Lucy hesitated, then visibly made a decision to speak her mind. "I know there are circumstances here you don't want to discuss with just anyone, but wouldn't it have been better to announce the engagement formally and get on with the wedding plans as if this were your ordinary, garden-variety, happy occasion?"

"I wasn't ready to say anything," Katie said stubbornly. She hadn't known what to say, if the truth be told. She was afraid she'd give away every blasted detail of her contract with Luke if she opened her mouth at all.

Lucy studied her worriedly. "Katie, maybe you shouldn't go through with it. Obviously you have serious reservations about marrying Luke. It's written all over your face."

"I have no reservations. I love him," Katie said grimly. "That's all that matters."

"No, it's not and you know it," Lucy countered. "You deserve more than some weird business bargain. Katie, you're the most honest, most straightforward person I know. You won't be able to live with yourself if you have to lie to everyone. It's no way to start a marriage."

"This arrangement is between Luke and me, no one else. We'll make it work."

"How?"

Katie lost patience. She was doing her best here. She didn't need her closest friend trying to sabotage her efforts. "Dammit, Lucy, I'm beginning to be sorry I ever told you the truth."

Lucy promptly looked chagrined. "Oh, sweetie, I'm sorry. I just want you to be as happy as I am."

Katie hugged her. "I will be. You'll see. Now scoot on out of here before Peg gets in. I have to tell her before the lunch crowd shows up and starts blabbing about the news."

"Good luck. You're going to need it. I remember when we were kids Peg could always see straight through you."

"Then I'll just have to do the best acting job of my entire life."

Unfortunately, she never had the chance. Within seconds after Peg's arrival—in fact while she was still tying an apron around her waist and Katie was gathering her courage—Luke strolled in the door of the diner. Katie guessed at once from his smug expression that he had heard that the news of their engagement was finally out. He was bound to figure that Peg would have heard it as well. In fact, he was making a beeline straight for her aunt. Katie rushed to intercept him.

Before she could get in a cautionary word, he smiled broadly at Peg, slipped an arm around Katie's waist and said, "So what did you think of our news?"

"News?" Peg had said, looking suspiciously from one to the other.

Katie jammed an elbow into Luke's side, but he kept that smile and his arm firmly in place and said, "The wedding, of course. You will be there, won't you? I know Katie's counting on you."

He dropped a perfunctory kiss in the vicinity of Katie's mouth, something he'd gotten into the habit of doing despite her protests.

"Gotta run," he said, still oblivious to the fact that he'd just dropped a bombshell. "I'll leave you two to finalize the rest of the plans."

He was gone before Katie could muster the strength to murder him, before she could recover from that slap-dash kiss, for that matter. Still a little weak-kneed, she turned to Peg, who was regarding her with an expression filled with hurt and dismay.

Before Katie could open her mouth, Peg shook her head, then whirled and went into the kitchen, where she stubbornly remained for the rest of Katie's shift.

Faced with her aunt's obvious disapproval and consumed with guilt, Katie didn't have the courage to force a confrontation. She slipped away from the diner as soon as her replacement came in and drove out to the beach. It was where she'd always gone when she needed to think.

She headed straight for her favorite secluded bench, drew her knees up to her chest and huddled there trying to figure out how to handle the mess she seemed destined to make of her life.

Today, though, the soothing sound of the surf, the scent of salt air and pine, was lost on her. She kept thinking of the hurt in Peg's eyes, the worry in Lucy's expression, and her own terrible doubts, which were mounting with every hour that passed.

It wasn't as if anything had changed during the past few weeks since the decision had been made. She and Luke still maintained a cautious distance. Their conversations about the wedding were so matter-of-fact she'd found herself grinding her teeth every time she thought about them.

How could something she'd prayed for most of her life be making her and everyone around her so thoroughly miserable? Was Lucy right? Was marrying Luke for all the wrong reasons the worst mistake she would ever make? Could she survive day after day, living a charade with Luke and hiding her true feelings from him?

So far, he'd certainly lived up to his part of their bargain. He'd deposited ten thousand dollars into her bank account the very afternoon they'd reached an agreement. He'd negotiated a price on the new roof with Ron and had somehow managed to get workers on the job within days.

Maybe it would be good to have a brisk, no-nonsense financial whiz in charge of the business aspects of running the boarding house, she told herself consolingly. She had never been wild about maintaining the books, anyway. She was better at creating a homey, welcoming, family atmosphere. It seemed, in that regard at least, that she and Luke were a match made in heaven. And Robby, well, Robby was the bonus, the icing on the cake. Kate already knew that being his mother was going to fulfill all her fantasies. He was a terrific little boy and he'd accepted her more eagerly than she could have hoped.

Suddenly, as if just thinking about him had conjured him up, she felt Luke's presence. He settled himself onto the bench beside her, as he had so often in the past, slouched down, legs sticking straight out, arms stretched across the back of the bench, fingertips just barely brushing her bare shoulder. Her entire body heated from that innocent, casual touch. Katie longed to fling herself into his arms seeking the safe haven she had once found there. Instead, sitting stiffly, she waited for him to explain why he'd come.

He regarded her worriedly. "What's up, Katie? You look as if you've just lost your best friend."

She glanced over at him. He was dressed once again in the familiar, casual attire he'd always worn. She still couldn't reconcile this Luke with the man whose picture had appeared on so many financial pages, all decked out in perfectly tailored designer suits. This look made him seem familiar, accessible. She could almost believe he was still her best friend and that nothing had ever gone awry between them.

"How'd you find me?" she asked.

"Peg said you'd taken off. You weren't at the boarding house. After that it was easy. I spent a lot of years tracking you down every time you were hurting. You always aimed straight here, even when you were too young to drive and had to walk all the way." His gaze searched her face. "So what's the deal? Are you hurting now? And why was Peg in such a snit? She practically bit my head off."

"I'm feeling guilty."

"About?"

"The way Peg found out about our plans. That also explains her mood."

He regarded her with obvious puzzlement. "I thought you had told her. Isn't that how word got out today?"

She gave him a rueful look. "No, I didn't tell her. You did."

"Me? But I didn't say a word, not until..." He studied her expression, then groaned. "Hell, Katie, hadn't you told her before I showed up this afternoon? Half the town was talking about it by then. I just assumed..."

"Believe me, I know. I suppose it's better that the news came from you, rather than some well-meaning busybody," she said wearily. "Luke, she's so hurt. She hasn't said a single word to me."

His expression turned incredulous. "You mean you didn't sit down and talk about it after I left?"

"Not a word. She went into the kitchen and stayed there."

"No wonder she looked at me the way she did. Why didn't you go after her?"

"The diner was too busy," she said defensively.

Luke regarded her with blatant skepticism. In the face of his doubtful expression, Katie hesitated, then finally admitted the truth. "I'm afraid she'll guess. I'm afraid she'll take one look at my face and know that this whole thing is some sort of sick joke."

Luke stared at her for what seemed an eternity. "Is that how you see what we're doing?" he asked, his voice flat.

"Well, isn't it? Usually two people get married because they're madly in love, not because one wants a baby-sitter and the other one needs financial backing."

Apparently the bitterness she was feeling came through in her tone, because Luke asked quietly, "Do you want out of our deal, Katie? Is that what this is all about?"

"Yes," she said without thinking, then sighed. "No."

"Which is it?"

I want you to love me, she thought, but she didn't say the words aloud. There was no point in voicing the impossible. It would just make an already awkward situation untenable.

"We made a bargain. I intend to keep it," she said firmly, trying to blink back the tears that threatened.

For a minute Luke looked as if he might argue with her, but then his expression shut down. He reached over and gently brushed away the single tear that tracked down her cheek. "We'll make it work, Katie. I swear to you that somehow we'll make it work."

His solemn promise only served to make even more tears well up. Katie hurriedly swiped them away before they became a deluge.

When she could bear to meet his gaze, she looked up at Luke. "Thanks for coming to look for me. I needed a pep talk."

He gave her one of his patented, reassuring smiles. "In just a few more days, I'll be around whenever you need me. Don't forget that."

"I'm counting on it." She gave him a wobbly, damp smile. "By the way, why did you come if you didn't know about Peg and me?"

"Maybe I just wanted to see you," he said lightly.

Katie didn't believe that for a minute. "Is there a problem?"

"No, there is not a problem," he said with a touch of impatience. "I just had some time. I thought maybe we could go for a drive or something."

It was the first time she could think of that Luke had so much as hinted at a desire to spend time alone with her. Katie was certain there had to be more to it. "You and me and Robby?"

"No, Katie. You and me. Period." He shook his head. "I guess it was a bad idea."

Something in his expression told her she really had spoiled what had been meant as a gesture to bring them closer together before the wedding. "We could still go."

"You need to talk to Peg. At the moment that's more important. I know how much her opinion matters to you."

"She raised me, Luke. She's all the family I have." Suddenly something occurred to her. "Speaking of family, you haven't said a word about Tommy. Will your brother be here for the wedding?"

"No," he snapped without hesitation.

The curt response startled her. "Luke?"

"Leave it alone."

Something in his expression told her to do exactly as he asked. She knew Luke had been deeply hurt when Tommy had run off years ago, but surely after all this time he had forgiven him. He had adored his younger brother. No matter how many scrapes Tommy had gotten in, Luke had always bailed him out. In some ways, she suspected, Luke had even envied Tommy his rebellious ways.

Maybe she could find Tommy and lure him to the wedding, she thought briefly before assessing Luke's forbidding expression again. Then again, maybe she'd better stay away from that troubled relationship until she understood it. Besides, she had her own family emergency to resolve.

"I guess I'd better go find Peg and face the music," she said reluctantly.

"It'll be all right. She loves you. She just wants you to be happy."

Katie didn't have the heart to tell him that *that* was the problem. Peg wouldn't believe in a million years that Luke Cassidy could make her happy, not after he'd done such a bang-up job of breaking her heart.

* * *

At four-thirty in the afternoon the diner was usually empty. The lunch crowd was long gone. The school kids had finished their soft drinks, milk shakes and ice cream cones and headed home. And the dinner crowd, always light during the week, anyway, wouldn't show up for a good hour or more.

Peg usually used the time to check the day's receipts, make lists of supplies to be ordered or simply to put her feet up for a few minutes and catch a quick, refreshing nap before the chaos started all over again.

Today, however, Katie found her aunt pacing from the front door to the kitchen and back again, clearly distracted and upset. Watching her through the window, Katie sighed as she tried to gather the courage to go in. Finally, fearing she was about to be spotted anyway, she opened the door.

When the bell over the door rang, Peg glanced through the pass-through window from the kitchen and saw her. The worry lines in her forehead deepened as she came through the swinging door. Normally an energetic whirlwind, today her aunt looked her age. Her steps had slowed. Her usually tidy, short, gray hair was virtually standing on end from the number of times she'd dragged her fingers through it.

"There you are," she said quietly. "Where'd you go? To the beach?"

Katie grinned sheepishly. No one, with the possible exception of Luke, knew her better than this woman who had taken her in and loved her for so many years. "Where else?" she said.

"Feeling lousy?"

There was an accusation behind the question that Katie couldn't mistake. She deserved to feel lousy and they both knew it. "I'm sorry I hurt you."

"Are you?"

"You know I am. I would never intentionally do anything to upset you."

"I always thought that was true," Peg said, as if she were no longer quite so certain. With her expression far more nonchalant than the situation called for, she inquired, "So, when's the wedding?"

Katie knew a loaded question when she heard one. If she could say six months from now or even a month from now, Peg might believe that the leaked news truly was fresh and that she hadn't intentionally been shut out. When she heard the truth, she was going to be hurt all over again.

"Saturday," Katie said, watching the pain gather in Peg's eyes. "Justice of the Peace Abernathy is going to perform the ceremony at eleven o'clock."

Peg simply stared at her, shock written all over her face. "A justice of the peace? This Saturday? When exactly had you planned to get around to letting me know? After the honeymoon?"

As soon as the angry words were out, Peg Jones moved like a whirlwind. With brisk efficiency, she slapped a Closed sign on the door, poured two cups of coffee, plunked them on the counter and ordered Katie to sit.

"Okay. What's this all about?" the fifty-year-old woman demanded, her gaze pinned on Katie.

Katie winced under that penetrating look. She tried valiantly to put a positive spin on things. "Luke asked me to marry him. I said yes. It's as simple as that."

"Nothing's ever been simple between the two of you," Peg countered. "Katie, the man broke your heart. I've watched you mope around for the past six years, refusing to look at anyone else, shutting yourself off from life. Now he waltzes back into town, says let's get married and bingo, everything's just dandy again? I don't believe it. Has he even explained why he left? Has he apologized?"

"He doesn't owe me an apology."

Peg sniffed indignantly, but made no comment.

"Luke and I were . . . are best friends. I can't think of a better basis for marriage," Katie said defensively. "No two people could possibly know each other any better than Luke and I do. We're well suited. We know exactly what we're getting into."

She ignored the coffee her aunt had poured, stood and began cleaning the counter, which had already been polished to a shine. She didn't care. She needed to stay on her feet. She needed to be able to avoid her aunt's probing looks and pointed questions.

No matter how much her evasions hurt her aunt, Katie refused to admit out loud that Luke wasn't marrying her for love. She refused to admit that they had simply made a deal. That was no one's business, not even her beloved aunt's. Peg, who'd raised Katie to abide by an old-fashioned set of values and a romantic's notions of what marriage was supposed to be, would be appalled if she discovered the truth. Her own marriage to Katie's father's brother had been cut short by a tragic accident, but Peg's memories of that time had always brought a sparkle to her eyes.

"Hogwash," Peg said in response to Katie's claim. "Friendship has its places, but what about love, Katie? I've always dreamed of watching you walk down the aisle with a radiant look on your face. Friendship doesn't make you radiant. That takes fire and passion."

Katie thought back to the one night she'd spent in Luke's arms. There had been fire and passion enough that night. Loving him had been everything she'd ever imagined it could be. It had been ... she searched for a word adequate to describe it. *Magical,* she decided finally. The stuff of storybooks and romantic movies, certainly an equal to whatever Peg had shared with Harry Jones.

Losing Luke had been worse than anything Katie had ever dreamed of, especially without knowing why he had gone. That she'd been abandoned not just by a lover, but by a best friend had tormented her for the past six years. The loss had made her question her memories of that night, made her doubt herself in ways that she could never share, not with anyone.

Then, when she had seen Luke sitting in the back of the church at Lucy Maguire's aborted wedding ceremony, holding a handsome boy with the classic Cassidy features and Luke's unmistakable blue eyes, she had guessed at once why Luke had left Clover. He had gone away to marry the mother of that darling child. The only thing left to figure out had been where the boy's mother was now.

Naturally everyone in town had asked about Robby's mother, about the secret bride that no one—not even his very best friend—had known that Luke had taken.

And Katie had heard back from most of them, in the form of idle gossip at Peg's, gossip that usually turned silent the instant anyone noticed Katie's presence. No one had learned a blasted thing. Luke had remained discreetly tight-lipped on that score, except to say that he and the boy's mother were divorced. End of story.

Katie sighed. She doubted he would say anything more to her even if she tried to force the issue. That had always been Luke's way. He'd kept his emotions bottled up inside. He'd watched his mother get old and tired very quickly after his father split. He'd been more father than big brother to that hellion of a brother of his, and Tommy had paid him back by taking off just like their father. Katie had been the only one in town who'd detected the anguish that Tommy's leaving had caused Luke. Everyone else had said good riddance, but Luke had viewed Tommy's departure as his own failure. He had blamed himself for not being a good enough surrogate father, even though only a few years had separated him in age from Tommy.

She thought about that now and realized that despite his unexplained departure from her life, in her heart she had never doubted Luke's decency. It was at the core of who he was, a decent, responsible man, determined to be more honest and honorable than the father who'd abandoned him. She didn't believe for an instant that those two traits had vanished. He might not be in love with her. He might not have made the most romantic proposal on record. But he would do his very best to make her a good husband. He would honor this commitment he was making. And he'd come to her, chosen *her* because he wanted to do what was best for his son. That wasn't the act of a man who'd suddenly turned selfish.

Somehow she had to convince her aunt of that or Peg would be worrying herself sick.

She took her aunt's hand. "Please, Peg, I know it's unexpected—"

"A pure bolt out of the blue is more like it. He's only been back in town off and on for a couple of months now."

"Since March," Katie corrected.

"Whatever. I didn't even think the two of you were speaking."

"Well, obviously we are. This is what I want. What Luke and I want." She leaned across the counter to hug her aunt. "Please, I really need your support and your love. I need you to give us your blessing. You'll be there on Saturday, won't you? I can't possibly have a wedding without you."

"If I thought that were true, I'd stay away just to prevent you from making a terrible mistake," her aunt said.

"You can't protect me forever. I'm a grown woman. If this is a mistake, it's mine to make. I love him with all my heart, Peg. You know that. I always have. I have to try. I don't want to live with even more regrets."

"Regrets aren't always the worst things to have," her aunt argued. "But..." She cut off whatever she'd been about to say and sighed. "Never mind. I love you. If you can look me in the eye and tell me you think Luke will make you happy, then of course I'll be there."

Katie thought at first that her aunt's words were the concession she'd been seeking. One look into Peg's eyes told her otherwise. Her aunt meant them as a challenge.

"Well," Peg prodded.

Katie forced herself to meet her aunt's skeptical gaze. "I wouldn't be marrying him if I didn't believe that with all my heart," she said staunchly.

The firmly spoken words clearly didn't banish all of Peg's doubts, but she nodded, her expression resigned.

"Okay, then. Let's make some plans. I'll throw the reception for you afterward. Nothing fancy," she added quickly in response to Katie's frown. "Just a few folks over for a nice brunch at the house. Maybe a champagne toast."

"But..."

Peg waved off any objections. "I don't care how small the ceremony is or how rushed, every couple should start life with a few good wishes from their family and friends."

Katie figured her wedding day was going to be difficult enough without having to pretend in front of a bunch of people that it truly was the happiest day of her life. "I'll have to ask Luke," she hedged. "We really wanted to keep this simple and private."

"Can I give you one last piece of advice before I turn you over to that man?" Peg asked. She didn't pause long enough for a reply, which Katie didn't have ready, anyway. "You don't ask him for his opinion on every little thing, Katie. You tell him what you want once in a while."

Good advice, Katie thought, as she gave a last swipe at the diner's counter before racing home to do the Monday laundry for the boarding house. But how was she supposed to tell Luke Cassidy that the only thing she really wanted from him was his love?

Chapter Two

On the night before her wedding, when most brides would be celebrating with a rehearsal dinner or a shower, Katie gathered the residents of the Clover Street Boarding House in the living room. She'd learned that afternoon that they were all terrified about what her marriage would mean to the future of the boarding house. Seventeen-year-old Ginger, who'd chewed her nails down to the quick again for the first time in months, had revealed the concerns of the half-dozen boarders.

"Katie, you haven't said. How soon will you be wanting us to leave?" Ginger had asked, her voice trembling with emotion. She'd been drying the same soup bowl for the past ten minutes, obviously trying to work up the courage to get into this with Katie.

Katie had stared at her blankly. "Leave? Who said anything about your leaving?" Understanding dawned. "Oh my heavens, is that why I've seen Mrs. Jeffers with the classifieds every evening this week? She's been going through them for the rest of you?"

"She's been looking for rooms to let, but there aren't any," Ginger had said, suddenly tearful. "We wondered how long you'd give us before we have to go?"

"Nobody's going anywhere," Katie had replied grimly, taking both the soup bowl and dish towel from the teenager's hands. "Have all of the others in the living room tonight at seven."

Looking hopeful, Ginger had rushed from the room, yelling at the top of her lungs.

Now all of the residents were sitting quietly, watching Katie. She could see the anxiety etched on their faces.

There was Mrs. Jeffers, of course. She'd been the first to move in, a month after her husband had died. She had a starchy, prim demeanor that covered the fact that she feared no one would accept her now that she was no longer part of a couple. Once someone breached that reserve, though, the sixty-five-year-old widow had a wicked sense of humor and endless compassion and energy.

Ginger had followed. She'd been fifteen, a runaway who'd never said one single word about the past she'd left behind. For a while she had shared a room with Ron Mathews's sister, Janie. The two of them had formed a bond that had been wonderful to witness. And both of them had come to adore Mrs. Jeffers, who'd quickly become a surrogate grandmother to both teens. Janie still stayed with them whenever she came home from college.

John O'Reilly, with his round, jovial face, rimless spectacles and fringe of white hair, reminded them all of Santa Claus. A retired fireman, he'd volunteered to do the grocery shopping for Katie. She suspected he'd done it so he could stock the kitchen with his favorite snacks. Hardly a night passed that he wasn't in there at midnight with a bowl of ice cream, popcorn or, in the summertime, a peach cobbler he'd made himself and shared with the others at dinner.

When Sophie Reynolds and her daughter had moved out after Sophie's wedding, her room had been quickly let to dark-haired, energetic Teresa Parks, a young woman in her early thirties who'd just taken a secretarial job at the bank. She'd come home to Clover after a bitter divorce she never discussed. She'd told Katie only that she needed time to get back on her feet before finding a house of her own.

The remaining tenant at the moment was a salesman, in town for just a few days. Katie noticed that Dennis Brown had gone straight to his room after dinner and hadn't come back down for this meeting. It was hardly surprising since he'd be moving on first thing in the morning, right before the wedding that had thrown everyone into such a tizzy.

Just as Katie was about to start the meeting, the front door opened. Luke strolled in with Robby bounding ahead of him. An immediate silence greeted their arrival.

"Luke, what a surprise!" Katie said. She hadn't realized, in fact, that he'd brought Robby over from Atlanta where he'd been finishing up kindergarten. She'd assumed he would remain there with Luke's housekeeper until after the wedding. "What are you doing here?"

"I heard you were having a meeting with the tenants tonight. Since I'll be moving in any day now, I thought I should sit in, too. And I thought it was about time everyone got to meet my son."

"Who told you about...?" Katie began, but stopped when she saw the guilty flush in Ginger's cheeks. "Well, it doesn't matter."

She gave everyone a reassuring look as Luke found a vacant seat and pulled Robby onto his lap. "I called this meeting tonight because I wanted to reassure you that my marriage won't change anything around here."

Unfortunately her words appeared to have little effect. In fact, every blasted person at the room was staring not at her, but at Luke, whose expression suddenly seemed excessively dark and forbidding.

"Isn't that right, Luke?" she prodded pointedly, praying that he wouldn't launch into some list of changes he intended to make.

She knew he'd been making notes for the past month, hunching over her books, hovering over her as she worked, examining every nook and cranny of the place and jotting down needed repairs. So far he'd kept silent about his thoughts on the boarding house operation, but Katie knew it was only a matter of time before he would feel compelled to seize control of the place. To a man like Luke, taking charge was as natural as breathing.

"Luke, no one has a thing to worry about," she stated emphatically. "Isn't that right?"

"For now," he said.

It was hardly the enthusiastic endorsement Katie had hoped for. For some reason, though, it seemed to do what her own promise had not. Everyone nodded happily.

"It's going to be real nice to have a handsome young man in the house," Mrs. Jeffers said. Katie glanced at Luke. Before he could respond to the compliment he clearly assumed had been meant for him, the widow held out her arms to Robby, who deserted his father and bounded over to her without a hint of reservation. "I declare you are about the handsomest boy I have ever seen."

Robby grinned, his smile so exactly like Luke's that Katie's breath caught in her throat. She couldn't tell from Luke's expression if he was laughing at his own mistake or was simply pleased to see Robby being welcomed so warmly.

"Will you be my grandma?" Robby asked Mrs. Jeffers. "My real grandmas died."

"I would be honored to be your grandma," Mrs. Jeffers said, looking pleased as punch.

"You smell nice, like flowers," Robby announced.

Mrs. Jeffers, whose own grandchildren lived on the West Coast, beamed at Katie. "Dear, I do believe this is going to work out rather well."

The others nodded in agreement. Katie wished she were half so certain.

As the meeting at the Clover Street Boarding House ended with one of Mr. O'Reilly's fresh fruit cobblers being dished up and served to everyone, Luke gave Ginger a suspicious wink that had Katie crossing the room in a flash.

"Thanks for letting me know," he said as Katie joined them.

She was just in time to overhear him and guess that he was referring to tonight's meeting. If that hadn't confirmed her earlier suspicion, Ginger's blushing cheeks would have.

"It was no big deal. I just figured if you were going to be living here, you should be a part of it," Ginger said, evading Katie's gaze. "See you. I've got studying to do."

"My, my, another conquest," Katie observed, unable to curb her irritation with Luke's intrusion into her meeting. "What did you do to win her over? Offer to buy her a new car? Maybe pay her way through college?"

Luke, blast him, refused to rise to the taunt. He grinned at her indignant tone. "You're the only one around here I'm buying off, Katie. Swear to God."

Swear to God. Those were the words Luke had always used to convince her that he was being totally honest. He tended to use them loosely, which somewhat dimmed their ability to reassure.

"Buying off?" she repeated lightly. "I made a legitimate business deal. That's all."

His grin remained unrepentant. "Then you must be afraid you're losing your grip around here. Is that what's made you so cranky and suspicious all of a

sudden?'' he inquired in that lazy, amused tone that
set Katie's teeth on edge.

Before she could reply, he gestured to Mrs. Jeffers.
"Hey, darlin', would you mind keeping an eye on
Robby for a bit? I'd like to take Katie for a walk. She
needs to cool off.''

Given the fact that it was still ninety degrees outside, Katie assumed the remark had to do with her
temper, not the temperature.

Mrs. Jeffers, who'd apparently missed Luke's true
meaning or assumed it was some lover's ruse to get
Katie alone, beamed. "You two young people go right
ahead. Robby and I will play a game of checkers until
you get back. He tells me he's world-champion cali-
ber.''

Luke brushed a kiss on the woman's weathered
cheek, then whispered, "I hear you're the champ of
the boarding house. Go easy on him.''

Katie watched the teasing exchange with her irritation mounting by unreasonable leaps and bounds.
"Trying to rub salt in the wound?'' she inquired when
he'd propelled her outside.

"What wound would that be?''

"That you can take over here anytime you want.
You're obviously trying to win over Mrs. Jeffers. And
you already have Ginger reporting every move I make
to you." She paused on the front steps and frowned at
him. "How did you get her to spill the beans about
tonight's meeting, anyway?''

"I ran into her at the library. We got to talking. She
mentioned the meeting. It was hardly a sinister, pre-
meditated act of treason.''

Katie sniffed. "That depends on your point of view, I suppose. Just in case you've forgotten, let me remind you that we made a deal. You're not supposed to interfere with my tenants."

He regarded her with amusement. "What interference? I'm just being friendly. If we're all going to be living together, we need to get along, isn't that right?"

Thoroughly exasperated, Katie couldn't think of a single way to fault that logic. "I suppose," she said grudgingly. "I just want it on the record that I don't like what you did tonight."

"Showing up?"

"Taking over."

"Katie, I did not take over," he said reasonably. "Come on. Let's walk."

She followed him without argument, still seething over what had happened earlier, even though she suspected she might be overreacting just the teensiest bit. She blamed it on nerves over the wedding that was less than twenty-four hours away.

The truth was, though, if she didn't take a firm stand now, the next thing she knew Luke would be running her boarding house and she would be doing...what? She had no idea what she would do if she lost control of the boarding house.

Starting up that business, buying the old McAllister place and making a go of it had been the only thing that had saved her sanity after Luke had left town.

"You did, you know," she accused.

He regarded her as if he'd forgotten the argument. "Did what?"

"'Take over.'"

"Katie, I barely said two words."

"But those were the only words they listened to," she grumbled.

"Sweetheart..."

The endearment grated. "I am not your sweetheart. I'm your business partner."

"Okay, *partner.* It was only natural that they want to know where I stand. I'm marrying you. I'm moving in. I'm an unknown quantity, someone who could disrupt their lives. They wanted to hear straight from me what my role is going to be. What did you expect me to do?"

"You could have deferred to me," she said. "Maybe reminded them that it's still my boarding house, that you're only a silent partner, that you have other, more important fish to fry." Struck by an unexpected thought, she regarded him worriedly. "You do, don't you? You haven't retired or something?"

"Worried I'll be underfoot all the time tempting you to do wild, irresponsible things?"

Katie's pulse skipped a beat at the deliberate innuendo and its matching glint in Luke's eyes. "Hardly," she said.

Luke laughed, probably at her dead-giveaway, breathless tone. "Katie, stop worrying. Give them a week or two to get used to my presence and they'll be right back to relying on you for everything." He stopped under a streetlight and grinned at her.

"What?" she demanded.

"I just never noticed before how much you hate change. You're a control freak."

This from a man who'd manipulated her into marrying him, Katie thought. "I am not."

"You are. You're even more scared about tomorrow than I am, because you can't predict what will happen next."

His observation about her fears barely registered. She was too intrigued by the revelation he'd made about himself. "You're scared?" she asked doubtfully.

He didn't look frightened. He looked like a man with the confidence to take over the whole damned town of Clover if he had a mind to. For all she knew that was his devious intention. Maybe he'd just started with the boarding house, because he knew she'd be an easy mark.

Before she could work herself into a frenzy over what Luke might or might not be truly up to, he caught her off guard again by admitting to his fears straight out.

"Sure, I'm scared," he said. "It's not like I go around making deals like this all the time. It's a first for me, too."

Katie regarded him thoughtfully. "I guess I hadn't thought of it that way." She lifted her gaze to his and studied him intently, trying to assure herself that he was being totally truthful.

As if he'd guessed her intention, he smiled. "Swear to God, Katie."

Finally convinced, she grinned back at him. "Thanks."

"For what?"

"For knowing the right thing to say...again."

"I hope I always will."

He suddenly looked so sad, so filled with his own doubts that Katie very nearly stood on tiptoe to kiss him. She knew, though, that a quick, consoling brush of her lips across his would never satisfy her. It would be like playing with matches. And she had vowed that she would not risk the pain that was sure to follow.

"We'd better be getting back," she said instead, starting away from him.

"Katie?"

She turned back.

"There's something we should talk about," he began.

His tone sounded so ominous that Katie promptly decided she didn't want to hear whatever he was about to say. "Can't it wait?"

Luke looked torn. Clearly the idea of putting off whatever he'd been about to say was a relief, yet he seemed to be struggling with his conscience.

"It really shouldn't."

Now she knew for certain she didn't want to hear it. "Please, Luke. Can't we just enjoy the night, pretend we're any other couple about to get married in the morning, and put off all the problems until after the ceremony? Please?"

"I suppose that's not too much to ask," he agreed, that same mix of relief and reluctance in his voice.

He held out a hand and Katie slipped hers into it, letting his warmth and strength wash through her. They walked back to the boarding house hand in hand and for those few minutes, anyway, Katie forced away all of the doubts. If she closed her eyes, she could almost pretend that tomorrow was going to be the happiest day of her life.

"It's not going to work, big brother!"

Luke's fingers tightened around the phone. Just the sound of his brother's voice these days was enough to make his blood run cold. Tommy was the last person he'd wanted to hear from on his wedding day.

"What's not going to work?" he asked, even though he knew he wasn't going to like the answer.

"This farce of a marriage. You're only doing it to keep me from getting custody of Robby, aren't you? It's just another one of your cold-blooded plots to have everything your own way."

Despite Luke's automatic inclination to dismiss anything Tommy had to say, he couldn't deny that the accusation hurt. When had he become so cold-blooded and calculating? Luke had a feeling it went back to the day he had made his bargain with Robby's mother six years ago. From that moment on, knowing that he'd have to give up Katie to do what was right, his own soul had been in jeopardy. He would never give Tommy the satisfaction of admitting that, though.

"Whether I'm married or not, you don't have a snowball's chance in hell of getting custody of *my* son," Luke said icily. "Why don't you save yourself the cost of this suit?"

"Because Robby's mine, dammit."

"You abandoned him," Luke reminded him. "The minute Betty Sue Wilder told you she was pregnant, you took off. You never accepted responsibility for her or your baby. I did. I married Betty Sue so that Robby would have the Cassidy name, for whatever the hell it's worth.''

''Noble Saint Luke,'' Tommy said derisively. ''Always ready to jump in and clean up my messes, isn't that right? The truth was you were glad to marry Betty Sue. She was a hell of a lot hotter than any of the girls in your life.''

Luke thought of the one night he'd had with Katie, the night he'd never been able to put from his mind no matter how hard he'd tried. That night had overshadowed any experience he and Betty Sue had ever shared. Even now the memory made his blood turn hot. ''Shut up, Tommy.''

''You know it's true. That's why she left you, isn't it? Because you couldn't keep up with her.''

Luke kept a tight rein on his temper, but it was a costly effort. He could feel his pulse throbbing dully. ''Why don't you repeat some of your ugly opinions in court?'' he suggested. ''Let the judge see for himself exactly the kind of man you've turned out to be. The bottom line here isn't Robby. Not where you're concerned. You don't give a hoot about your son or what's best for him. If you did, you would never have filed this suit.''

''A boy should know his real daddy, don't you think so, big brother?''

''In most instances I'd agree with you. In this case I think your motives are highly suspect. You want me to pay you off to stay out of his life, don't you? That's what this is really about.''

''Is that what you think, big brother? That money can make up for losing a kid?''

''Tommy, I believe that you're the kind of man who'd sell his own mother for the right price. This interest in Robby was awfully sudden. You didn't seem to give a damn until you happened to catch that news report on my net worth.''

''Since we're into motives and honesty here,'' Tommy retorted, ''how does old Katie feel about being used? Does she know she's supposed to do the mom-and-apple-pie thing when you walk into court?''

Luke winced at that. He'd told Katie nothing at all about the circumstances of Robby's birth. Nor had he told her that Tommy was trying to take the boy away from him in what promised to be an ugly court case. And because of his international reputation, that case was likely to make news around the world.

Okay, so it was a lousy secret to be keeping. He hadn't told her up front because he'd been afraid she'd turn him down if she knew exactly what she was getting into. He'd almost told her last night, but he'd been all too willing to drop the issue when she'd asked him not to get into anything too heavy on the eve of their wedding.

Afterward once she'd had time to fall in love with Robby, once she thought of his son as her own, he prayed that she would be every bit as furious and indignant about Tommy's out-of-the-blue plans as he was.

Apparently his silence told Tommy all he needed to know. ''You haven't told her, have you? Poor old Katie. You're still taking her for granted, big brother.

One of these days that arrogance of yours is going to cost you big-time.''

It was the only thing Tommy had said that had the ring of gospel truth. Luke did take Katie for granted. He counted on her compassion, her generosity and the deep and abiding love she'd once given him so freely. One of these days, though, he would likely pay a terrible price for taking all that she had to offer and giving her nothing but lies in return. He was likely to lose the only woman he'd ever really given a damn about.

''Goodbye, Tommy.''

''See you in court, bro.''

Tommy's words were still ringing in his ears as Luke dressed for the wedding an hour later. He'd chosen his most formal suit, a black pin-stripe that had served him well in the business world. Maybe it would bring him luck today as well, more luck than he had any right to expect.

He thought back over the life he'd managed to put together despite his unfortunate marriage to Betty Sue Wilder. He'd mastered finance while living in Atlanta, turning an understanding of basic accounting into an intuitive grasp of the corporate bottom line.

Between his careful personal financial management and his genius for investments, he'd parlayed a generous salary into the kind of wealth he'd never even imagined growing up back in Clover. His tight-fisted control of the bankbook had irritated the daylights out of his wife and had, no doubt, contributed to her decision to take off. Betty Sue hadn't liked being hemmed in by anything as mundane as a budget.

Luke, however, had held the opinion that having money one day didn't guarantee he'd have it the next. He spent it as if each dollar might be his last. He would never, ever be left in the sorry financial mess that had faced his mother after his father took off.

He'd been horrified upon returning to Clover to see the kind of risks Katie had taken with her own financial stability. It was too late for him to do anything for his mother, but Katie's situation at least was about to change. He'd have her on a sound financial footing in no time... if she would listen to him. She probably wouldn't, he admitted with a sigh. For the hundredth time he wondered why he had been so hell-bent on making this particular bargain. He knew he could have fought off his brother's claim to Robby on his own. He could have hired a nanny to look after the boy.

But from the moment he'd realized that Tommy intended to fight him for Robby's custody, Luke's head had been filled with thoughts of Caitlyn. Six years ago he'd chosen duty over his heart. The decision to marry Betty Sue had been forced on him by a deeply ingrained sense of honor. Afterward, he had grimly set out to erase all of his most precious memories of Katie.

A few months ago, with Betty Sue gone and Tommy raising cain about the son Luke had stolen from him, Luke had just as systematically set out to learn all he could about Katie's life since he'd left Clover.

And then he'd formed his plan for getting her to marry him. He'd gone about it with the kind of dogged determination and attention to detail that had made him a success in business. Major corporate mergers had been achieved with less rigorous planning.

Not once had it occurred to him to simply court her. For one thing, there wasn't enough time. For another, he'd always figured the sensible, straightforward approach was best. Most people understood dollars and cents in ways they couldn't comprehend emotions.

Caitlyn had readily confirmed his beliefs on that score. She'd seen right away that what he was suggesting would work out best all around. Hell, she'd even laid out a damned payment plan for her commitment. Ten thousand a year for five years! He'd been stunned by her audacity. He'd also admired it in a grudging sort of way.

The one thing he couldn't figure out for the life of him, though, was why her quick response had left him feeling empty and somehow disappointed.

"You never said. Is Katie going to be my new mommy? I mean is that what I should call her?" Robby asked, tugging at his tie interrupting his thoughts. His own suit was an exact replica of Luke's, but he was clearly less comfortable in it.

He was far more fascinated with the concept of having a new mother. He rarely saw Betty Sue, which was her choice, not Luke's and certainly not Robby's. For weeks after she'd gone Robby had stood silently in front of her photograph, tears rolling down his cheeks.

Now, he asked Luke, "Would Mommy be mad if I called Katie Mommy, too?"

"I think she'd want you to do whatever made you happy," Luke said.

Robby frowned. "But will Katie mind? I mean I'm not really her little boy."

"That's something you and she will have to decide."

"Will we live in her house? I like it there. Mrs. Jeffers said I could call her Grandma, and I beat her at checkers. And it won't be lonely with all those people around all the time."

Luke felt as if he'd been sucker punched by Robby's calmly delivered statement. No five-year-old should be talking about loneliness so matter-of-factly.

There was no question that Robby had spent far too much time alone in his young life. Betty Sue hadn't been much interested in mothering. She'd had a list of available baby-sitters that would just about have filled his Rolodex and she hadn't hesitated to call them morning, noon or night. As a result, Robby was amazingly adaptable and outgoing, almost desperate in his bids for approval. Some of those traits would benefit him, Luke supposed, but that knowledge didn't assuage his guilt.

"It will be like getting a big family all at once, won't it?" Luke said, wondering again at the odd sense of disappointment that had settled into the region of his heart.

What kind of privacy would a pair of newlyweds have in a crowded boarding house? And how long would it be before everyone in town knew that he and Katie were sleeping in separate bedrooms, as she'd dictated?

Of course, if every room were rented ...

A slow grin crept across his face. Yes, indeed, that would solve that particular problem in a hurry. Katie couldn't very well hold him to their deal if there was a paying customer for that extra bedroom. He swore to himself that he'd have that situation resolved by the time they came back from their farce of a honeymoon in Charleston. He'd sensed an ally in Mrs. Jeffers. Perhaps she would be willing to screen new applicants for the room. The whole matter could be handled in no time.

For some reason the thought of Caitlyn in his bed, in his arms, warmed him in a way that nothing else had in a very long time. He couldn't think of a single other business merger that had affected him quite the same way, a fact that would have surprised his ex-wife. She'd always thought the only thing that turned him on was business. He hadn't been able to deny it...until now.

Now it seemed that his best friend, the woman he was supposedly marrying solely for convenience, had the ability to make his whole damned body throb with anticipation. Something told him this marriage was going to turn out to be a whole lot more than he'd bargained for.

Chapter Three

Lucy Maguire Ryder, who was the only person who knew the whole truth about this sham of a wedding, stood back and studied Katie speculatively. The close scrutiny had Katie squirming. She was nervous enough without her best friend looking her over with the intensity of the last quality control inspector on the assembly line at General Motors.

"You look beautiful," Lucy declared finally, when she had straightened the hem of Katie's new knee-length silk dress for the tenth time in the past fifteen minutes.

"Yes, you do, darling," Peg agreed. "That pale pink brings out the roses in your cheeks, though why you wouldn't agree to a fancy gown is beyond me.

This is your wedding, hopefully the only one you'll ever have. You should have all the trimmings.''

"Wedding gowns are outrageously expensive," Katie said. She didn't add that the boarding house debts had eaten up all of her savings. Such an admission might lead the conversation too close to her financial arrangement with Luke.

"I could have made one for practically nothing," Peg began.

Katie quickly cut her off. "There was no time for you to make it and there was no point in spending all that money for a ceremony that will take five minutes," she countered. "Luke and I agreed this was more sensible."

"Sensible," Peg repeated with a huff. "Weddings aren't supposed to be sensible. People in love should indulge themselves just this once."

Katie exchanged a look with her best friend and tried to avoid her aunt's penetrating gaze.

"What?" Peg exclaimed, catching the two of them. Her forced cheerfulness died, replaced at once by suspicion. "What is it that you're keeping from me? From the very beginning, I've suspected that you weren't telling me the whole truth. Now what's going on here?"

"Nothing," Katie reassured her, giving her a hug. "Thank you for everything."

Peg glanced from Katie to Lucy and back again, clearly not satisfied. Finally, apparently guessing that she wouldn't learn anything from either of them, she shrugged. "Everything? I have a cake and a few canapés at home. I always dreamed of—"

"Stop it," Katie said firmly, before Peg had them all in tears with her description of the ideal church wedding she'd envisioned for her niece. "This is what I want—just a quiet ceremony with the people I love most. Isn't that what really matters?"

To Katie's relief, the question, for which there was only one reasonable answer, finally silenced her aunt's litany of regrets.

"I'm sorry," Peg said. "The last thing I want is to spoil this day for you." She reached into her handbag and pulled out a small package. "This is for you. It was your grandmother's."

Katie's throat clogged with emotion as she accepted it. She tugged the white ribbon free, then slid the box from its wrappings. Her fingers shook as she fumbled with the tight lid. When she finally had it open, she found a small, white leather-bound prayer book with her grandmother's name engraved in gold.

"She carried it at her wedding. It was a gift from your grandfather," Peg said.

Clasping the prayer book tightly, Katie threw her arms around her aunt and hugged her. "Thank you."

"I've been saving it all these years. Your mother and I both carried it at our weddings. Your mother wanted you to have it on your wedding day." Peg dabbed gently at the tears spilling down Katie's cheeks. "Don't cry, sweetheart. You'll ruin your makeup."

"Thank you," Katie whispered again.

"Stop that. You don't need to thank me for doing what your mother asked," Peg said brusquely, swiping at her own tears.

"I'm not thanking you for that," Katie protested. "I just want you to know how grateful I am for everything you've done for me. You took me in. You've been like a second mother, and no girl could have had a better one. I love you."

"Oh, baby." Peg's embrace tightened. "I love you, too."

With both of them about to dissolve into sentimental tears, Lucy stepped in. "Enough, you two, or Clover will be flooded by nightfall. Besides, we have a wedding to get to." She gave Katie's hand an encouraging squeeze. "All set?"

"As ready as I'll ever be."

It wasn't until she walked into Justice of the Peace Abernathy's dingy, cramped foyer a half hour later and heard the recorded sound of organ music that Katie recognized the exact consequences of the choice she'd made in her kitchen just a few short weeks earlier. Visions of all of the other lovely weddings in which she'd participated as a bridesmaid crowded into her head. This was... She couldn't find words to describe how depressing it all was, especially since she knew that she and Luke didn't even share the kind of love that might have conquered this inauspicious beginning.

Suddenly the enormity of what she was about to do struck her. For one fleeting instant she considered turning right around and running as fast and as far from Clover, South Carolina, and Luke Cassidy as she could get. She knew, though, that distance alone would never bring her peace of mind. For better or worse, this was the choice of her heart, if not her head.

"Are you okay?" Lucy asked in a hushed voice as Peg went in to take a seat.

"Peachy," Katie replied and wondered if the butterflies in her stomach could be squelched by sheer bravado. "Where's Luke?"

Lucy peered through the curtain that shielded the justice of the peace's office. "In with Mr. Abernathy. Robby's there, too. He looks so sweet. He's all dressed up just like his daddy. Peg's talking to them, but Luke keeps looking this way as if he's afraid you're about to bolt." Lucy regarded her intently. "You aren't, are you?"

Katie glanced longingly toward the front door, then sighed and shook her head as the organ music swelled and shifted into an enthusiastic rendition of the wedding march. Lucy squeezed her hand reassuringly.

"Show time, sweetie."

Katie drew in a deep breath and peeked through the archway into the room where she was about to be married. The clutter of dark antiques, the frayed upholstery and the heavy drapes were incredibly oppressive, hardly what she'd always imagined as the setting for her wedding. Before she could get too depressed, she brought herself up short. She was beginning to get as caught up as Peg on the frills, rather than focusing on what this day was really all about—a commitment to love, honor and cherish Luke Cassidy all the days of her life.

That much shouldn't be too difficult. She'd already had years of practice. If only he were coming to this ceremony with the same deep emotions, she thought wistfully. Well, there was no point in wishing for the impossible. This was the bargain she'd made and she intended to make the best of it.

Holding in a sigh of regret, she looked into that dreary office one more time. Robby was practically bouncing up and down with excitement. Luke's gaze was trained on the opening, as steady and confident as ever. Katie locked gazes with those familiar blue eyes and let them lure her into the room.

She was only dimly aware of what happened next. Mr. Abernathy read an unhurried version of the all-too-familiar ceremony. Katie hadn't been a bridesmaid more times than she could recall without learning the words by heart. She kept wishing he would get on with it. She wouldn't believe what she was doing— the emotional risk she was taking—until she and Luke had both said "I do" and the justice of the peace had pronounced them man and wife.

Man and wife! Her pulse thumped unsteadily at the thought. *All the days of our lives!* Dear heaven, was she out of her mind?

Just when she was about to panic, her gaze was inevitably drawn back to Luke's eyes. Now, with the weight of the vows spelled out, she thought she saw the same doubts and turmoil reflected in his clear blue eyes. Somehow it helped just knowing he was as nervous as she was.

Then suddenly he smiled, a slow, reassuring curve of his lips that unexpectedly calmed her. His mischievous wink had her smiling back at him.

And then, just when she was beginning to relax and enjoy it, the ceremony ended and she was wearing a simple gold band on the third finger of her left hand.

Luke examined its mate on his own finger with the same amazed expression she was sure was on her own face.

For the first time Katie actually looked around and registered the pleased expression on Lucy's face, the tears shimmering in Peg's eyes and the bouquet that Luke had awkwardly shoved into her hands right before the ceremony. It was an assortment of blue, yellow and white wildflowers that was so reminiscent of the first flowers he'd ever picked for her that it brought tears to Katie's eyes. She was probably the only bride in history who was choking back sobs of regret for lost dreams within seconds after saying "I do."

"You may kiss the bride," Mr. Abernathy said jovially, startling Katie and Luke out of their private thoughts.

Luke hesitated just long enough to force a flood of embarrassed color into Katie's cheeks. Then he dutifully swept her into his arms with a dramatic flourish meant to satisfy the handful of onlookers.

Though his enthusiasm for the task seemed obviously feigned to Katie, the touch of Luke's lips on hers for the traditional post-ceremony kiss made her pulse race with predictable ease. A wildfire of emotions sparked to life deep inside her, even though there wasn't anything the least bit passionate about the obligatory gesture. She hated her own quick response to what for Luke was merely a show for their small audience.

Robby's smacking kiss and tight hug, which promptly followed, were far more natural and enthusiastic. At least one of the Cassidy men seemed happy about the marriage, Katie thought bleakly.

Too bad it wasn't her new husband.

On the ride over to Peg's after the ceremony, Luke wondered at the quick burst of anticipation that had shimmered through him as he'd held Katie in his arms for that all-too-brief farce of a kiss. He glanced over at his bride, who was sitting stiffly beside him, looking more like someone going off to their own execution than a woman who was about to attend her wedding reception. Peg had insisted that Robby ride with her to give them time alone. Luke was beginning to regret accepting the gesture.

"I didn't have a chance to tell you earlier," he said quietly. "You look beautiful."

She regarded him skeptically. "I..."

"No protest," he said interrupting. "You do. You're the epitome of the radiant bride."

She still looked as if she wanted to argue the point, but this time she managed to say a polite thanks.

"Katie, if you don't start smiling, people are going to wonder if there was a shotgun at our backs today."

That drew a startled look. "What?"

"You know," he prodded. "A shotgun. A baby."

If he'd hoped to make her laugh at the absurdity of that, the attempt failed miserably. She frowned at him.

"Well, fortunately most people in Clover are very adept at counting to nine," she said. "When next March rolls around and there's no little Cassidy, they'll figure out they were wrong."

He sighed at her curt tone. "I wouldn't mind having another little Cassidy someday, yours and mine," he said quietly. "What about you?"

"Given the fact that I have no intention of sharing a bed with you that's going to be difficult to accomplish," she retorted without even a hint of hesitation.

He grinned at her certainty that she had that situation well in hand. "Oh, there are plenty of places to do the deed other than a bed. All it requires are two people with imagination and dexterity."

Suddenly the too-serious expression on her face faltered. A grin tugged at her resisting lips. Luke wanted a full-fledged smile.

"We could pull over and I could show you," he offered generously. "The back seat of a car is a very traditional place to start."

A smile broke at last. "In your dreams, Cassidy. We have a deal."

"I would be willing to sacrifice my credibility as an honest businessman by breaking this one clause in our bargain," he said.

Finally her eyes glinted with wicked amusement. "I could never ask such a thing of you."

"You're not asking," he protested, enjoying the tint of pink the teasing was putting back into her too-pale cheeks. "I'm offering."

"Save it for someone else."

"I don't expect to have another wife."

She nodded thoughtfully. "Then that is a problem, isn't it? It's a good thing the hot water heater at the boarding house rarely works. The cold showers will do you good."

Luke vowed to replace the hot water heater the minute they got back from their honeymoon. Meantime, he pulled into Peg's driveway and cut the engine. When Katie started to open her door, he reached across her, his arm brushing against her breasts, and closed it. She turned a startled look on him.

"What?"

"Before things get too crazy inside, I just want you to know..." He hesitated, uncertain what he could say that would express the strange mix of gratitude and unexpected anticipation he was feeling. "I know that most women look forward to their wedding day their whole lives. And I imagine this isn't anything like what you dreamed about."

"It doesn't matter," she said, though a slight trembling of her lower lip said otherwise.

"It does," he contradicted. "Despite the way this whole thing came about, Katie, from here on out I intend to live up to those vows."

The tears that suddenly welled up in her eyes were almost his undoing. He reached across and pulled her into his arms. "Don't cry, darlin', please."

"I...can't...help...it," she said haltingly between sniffs. "Oh, Luke, what if this was a terrible mistake? I don't think I could stand it if you ever regretted marrying me."

"No regrets. I guarantee it. And I'm going to do my damnedest to see that you don't have any, either," he said determinedly.

Katie unexpectedly giggled at that. "You sound so grim."

A rush of tenderness washed over him as he looked into her tear-streaked face. "I was going for reassuring," he said indignantly. "Now let's get inside before they send out a search party."

"I'm sure everyone inside is perfectly satisfied that they know exactly why we've been delayed," Katie said dryly.

She started once again to open the door.

"Stop that," Luke said. "Just this once will you stay still and wait for me to open the door for you, instead of bolting like you can't wait to get away from me?"

"Maybe I'm just anxious to get to the cake before you do."

"We have to cut that together," he reminded her. "It's a tradition."

He glanced into her eyes and saw at once that she recognized as well as he did the irony of worrying about a wedding cake tradition when they'd already turned the entire concept of marrying for love on its head.

The minute they walked through the door of Peg's familiar house, Luke felt as if he'd finally come home. As a boy he had spent more hours in this small, comfortable house with its sagging front porch and cheerful, haphazardly decorated rooms than he had at home.

And in more recent years, when the interior of his own house in Atlanta had been designed by some outrageously expensive decorator who was all the rage according to Betty Sue, he still hadn't felt as at ease as he did right here amid the hodge-podge of antiques and junk that Peg had lovingly assembled from past generations of her own family and her husband's.

Katie's own ancestors, he thought now, smiling at a memory. She had once taken him through the house and pointed out exactly which pieces had come from which relative. The furniture seemed to provide necessary and more tangible ties to her past than even the old photo album that Peg kept in a drawer of an antique, hand-carved, oak buffet.

But as familiar as everything was, today there was a distinct difference. Despite all the pleas he and Katie had made to keep things simple, the living room had been decorated with crepe paper streamers and glitter-encrusted wedding bells. A buffet table groaned under the weight of all the food Peg and the others had contributed for the occasion. In the middle sat a three-tiered wedding cake, lovingly iced and decorated with pink roses by Peg herself, he suspected. The miniature bride and groom on top were tilted slightly, as if they were as out of kilter as he felt.

The room had been filled with roses, which probably meant that every garden in Clover had been plundered for the occasion. Luke drew in a deep breath, inhaling that sweet scent, and wondered if he'd ever look at Katie and not imagine the tantalizing aroma of roses.

He glanced at her, and for the second time that day he caught the shimmer of unshed tears in her eyes. Guilt sliced through him. How could he have robbed her of the wedding—no, the marriage—that she deserved? He had to believe that given time he could make it up to her, that he could prove that she hadn't made a terrible bargain the day she'd agreed to marry him.

Don't forget the ten thousand dollars, a cynical little voice reminded him. It wasn't as if Katie was getting nothing from their deal. She had snapped up his offer of a financial bailout for the boarding house with only a token protest. Protest? Hell, she'd bargained with him for more. On balance, maybe they really did deserve each other and whatever misery today brought to each of them.

Still, he couldn't help responding to her threatened tears. He took her hand in his and squeezed it. Katie immediately turned a grateful smile on him.

"Ready?" She mouthed the single word silently.

He leaned down and whispered, "Whenever you are."

To hear the two of them bracing themselves to enter that living room and join the small celebration Peg had prepared, Luke swore anyone would have thought they were going into a battle they had no chance of winning.

Katie nodded, plastered a smile on her face that would have fooled ninety-nine percent of the population of Clover and drew him into the living room. Immediately, congratulatory cheers were called out by the gathering. Champagne toasts followed, led by Peg and echoed by all the women for whom Katie had served as bridesmaid. With each toast, Luke found himself wondering exactly what Katie had told her aunt about their relationship. Whatever she knew or suspected,

Peg had clearly decided to put on a front for Katie's sake.

That front lasted until everyone was absorbed with piled-high plates of country ham, potato salad, homemade biscuits and coleslaw. Then Peg clamped a hand around Luke's elbow and steered him from the room. She had a grip that had been strengthened by years of carrying trays of food and heavy coffeepots. He doubted he could have pried her loose with a crowbar. She didn't say a word until they were alone in the backyard. She settled onto one end of an old metal glider and waved him into the spot next to her.

"I'll be good to her," he vowed before Peg could say anything. He figured this was one of those situations that called for a preemptive strike. For an instant Peg indeed did look nonplussed, perhaps even a little relieved by his adamant declaration. Then her expression turned serious.

"Do you love her?" she asked.

"Peg, you know how I feel about Katie," he said evasively.

The vague statement had her expression clouding over. "There was a time when that was true, a time when I thought the two of you were destined to be married," she agreed slowly. "Then you ran off."

"There were circumstances . . ."

"Robby," she said bluntly.

He saw no point in lying. "Robby was a big part of it. I had a responsibility to him and to his mother."

"What about your responsibility to Katie?"

Luke sighed. He had never, *never* thought of Katie as a responsibility. She had been a gift, a treasure, the one constant in his life.

But because he had believed in honor and duty, he had walked away from her and done the only thing he could do. He had married his brother's lover, had accepted their child as his own. And because he loved Robby with all his heart, had loved him from the first instant he had set eyes on him, he had always thought of the blessings of that choice and not the sacrifices.

"The past is over and done with, Peg. I can't change it," he told her. "I can only do everything in my power to see that Katie is happy now."

Peg didn't seem totally placated by that, but she nodded. "See that you do," she said forcefully. "Or I swear, Luke Cassidy, I will see that you regret the day you ever hurt my girl a second time."

Luke had no idea how to respond to that, but it didn't matter because Katie opened the back door just then. Spotting them in the shade, she crossed the yard.

Looking from one to the other of them, she asked worriedly, "Is everything okay out here?"

Peg managed an astonishing transformation. She bestowed one of her warmest, sunniest smiles on her niece. "Everything is wonderful. Luke and I were just catching up a bit," she said, standing up and slipping her arm through Katie's. "Let's go back inside where it's cooler. It wouldn't do to have the bride looking all wilted when she's about to take off on her honeymoon."

Katie didn't seem reassured by Peg's cheerful demeanor. If anything, she looked even more concerned. Her gaze shot to Luke. He managed a smile every bit as broad and every bit as phony as Peg's.

"Let's cut the cake, darlin'," he said, looping his arm around her waist. "I doubt this day will get into the record books until somebody's snapped a picture of you shoving a slice into my mouth."

"Or into your face," Katie corrected thoughtfully. She gave him a dangerous look. "I do hope you've got some fancy hankies in that designer suit of yours."

Luke figured a faceful of cake would be a small price to pay for everything he'd ever done to Katie. Once she heard all of the reasons behind his decision to marry her, she was much more likely to come after him with a shotgun. As he recalled with some dismay, she was a damned good shot.

Chapter Four

The honeymoon promised to be a disaster. Katie saw the direction it was heading the minute Luke announced that they were going to Atlanta.

"Atlanta?" she'd repeated incredulously as they drove away from her aunt's house, tin cans clanging along behind the car. No wonder he'd been so blasted secretive about his plans. He had probably guessed exactly what sort of message he would be sending and how it would be received.

It made no difference to her that she'd been the first one to declare her bed off-limits. Until the moment he'd made his announcement, Katie realized she had been holding on to a false hope. She'd dreamed that once they were alone in some romantic setting for a few days the sparks that had once flown between them might be rekindled. She'd hoped the ensuing flames would send this coldly calculated marriage-of-convenience plan up in flames.

It hadn't been entirely wishful thinking on her part. Luke had made arrangements for Robby to stay with Aunt Peg, after all. She had taken that as a good sign. He could very well have insisted they bring his son along. Since this was hardly a traditional marriage, there didn't seem much reason to expect a traditional honeymoon, so why not include his son? And yet, he hadn't, which she had interpreted to mean something. Obviously, it did not.

Now Katie was forced to concede that even with Robby out of the picture, Luke had taken her at her stand-offish word. He apparently wasn't any more inclined than she had claimed to be to stir up any of those old sparks. He was taking her on what sounded to all intents and purposes like the perfect destination for a business trip. Worse, they were heading to the exact same city where he'd been living with his wife. In fact, for all she knew, they might be staying in the same house. The honeymoon wasn't exactly turning out to be the stuff of which dreams were made.

After a quick, disappointed scowl in Luke's direction, she fell silent. Apparently he got her message just as clearly as she'd received his. A dull red flush stole up his neck. He regarded her guiltily.

"Katie?" When she remained silent, he said, "This trip is just for show, right? We both understood that or at least, I thought we did. I figured I might as well take care of some loose ends, so I won't have to do it later."

"How efficient."

Despite her sarcasm, he smiled. "It won't be all business, I promise."

"Don't worry about me," she retorted, promptly making plans of her own to demonstrate how little it all mattered to her. "I have some friends in Atlanta I haven't seen in ages. I'm sure we can spend the next few days shopping and catching up."

His gaze narrowed suspiciously. "You hate shopping."

Katie shrugged, determined not to let him see how furious and hurt she was. "Maybe I'll like it better once I get the hang of it. Cee-Cee and Pris are grand masters. We're going to be here what? Three full days? Four? I figure we should be able to hit at least a mall a day."

"Cee-Cee and Pris? They sound like an act from some strip joint."

Despite her sour mood, Katie laughed at his assessment. "I'll have you know those names are short for Celeste Margaret Louise Pennington of the Birmingham Penningtons and Priscilla Elizabeth Warrenton of the Virginia Warrentons. Where they come from, they can call themselves anything they like and people will still be respectful, especially with all those gold credit cards in their purses."

"How on earth do you know old Cee-Cee and Pris?"

"They stayed at the boarding house summer before last and again last July. I think they were slumming it at first, but by the end of the first day, they fit right in. Cee-Cee has quite a knack in the kitchen. We ate Cordon Bleu-qualified meals for the entire week she was there both times. Mr. O'Reilly was taking notes like crazy. Mrs. Jeffers kept moaning about all the cholesterol, but she ate every bite, rich, creamy sauces and all. They could hardly wait for the girls to come back."

"Did Pris adapt to small-town life as well?"

"Pris spent her days attaining what she described as the very best tan of her entire life, then devoted her evenings to worrying about what her dermatologist would have to say about it. I think she might best be described as a conflicted personality. She could make split-second decisions about almost anything. Then she spent the rest of the time questioning herself. It was fascinating."

"I'll bet," Luke said, clearly bemused by her descriptions. "And you've stayed in touch with the two of them?"

"Absolutely. They're dying to come back later this summer." She glanced at him pointedly. "Of course, now there's no place to put them."

"That's easily solved. I'll just move in . . ."

Katie saw exactly where he was heading. Given the lack of seductive intent evidenced in his honeymoon arrangements, she thought he had one hell of a nerve suggesting they sleep together when they returned home.

"Don't even think about it," she warned. "And speaking of sleeping arrangements, I hope you've booked us into a suite with a very large sofa. Or will we be staying at the house you shared with your last wife?"

Luke flinched at the direct hit. "I sold that house before I left Atlanta," he said tersely. "I never liked it."

"I trust you got a good price."

He ignored the sarcasm once more. "Naturally since it's our honeymoon, I have booked us into the honeymoon suite. It has a very large bed." There was a wicked, challenging glint in his eyes as he said it.

"I'm sure I'll be very comfortable then," Katie said with satisfaction. "But you'd better check on that sofa."

"Katie..."

"I think I'll take a little nap," she said cheerfully. "Wake me when we get to Atlanta. I want to call Cee-Cee and Pris right away. Oh, and you might want to do something about those tin cans. They're giving me a headache."

She decided it was to Luke's credit that he didn't declare that he wouldn't mind if her whole stubborn head fell off. If he was irritated with her, though, it was too damned bad. She figured it made them just about even. She was flat-out furious with him.

Atlanta had been a very bad idea, Luke decided as he glanced over at his sound-asleep bride. Her light brown hair, which had been curled more than usual for the wedding ceremony, brushed her cheeks in wayward wisps. The light dusting of makeup she had endured for the occasion hadn't covered the faint smattering of freckles across her nose. Her mouth, still pink with a shade of lipstick more delectable than any he could ever recall her wearing, invited kissing. The scent of roses, either from a perfume or from the flowers that had filled Peg's house, clung to her. She looked fresh and innocent ... and furious, he admitted ruefully.

Katie was cranky as the dickens and rightfully so, he conceded. No woman, even one entering into a marriage with few illusions, wanted to hear that her honeymoon had been tacked on to a business trip. It was a tactical blunder on his part if ever there was one.

He reminded himself irritably that he was supposed to be cementing this marriage into some facsimile of the real thing. If he couldn't show a court that he and Katie were the ideal couple, who knew what some wayward judge might do about Robby's custody. Tommy was no prize, but he was the boy's natural father, albeit a single one. Luke had figured this marriage, along with Betty Sue's support, was going to give him a comfortable edge in the custody dispute. That could hardly work if he and Katie were glaring daggers at each other or, worse, not even speaking. And Tommy knew exactly how to wield that particular weapon in court. As he'd already threatened, he wouldn't hesitate to use it.

Beyond all of that, in the past few weeks, ever since Katie had declared her bed off-limits, Luke had been ridiculously obsessed with getting her into it. He couldn't even look at her without desire slamming through him. Aside from the pure frustration, it was getting to be damned uncomfortable. And wanting Katie this badly wasn't a complication he'd considered when he'd selected her for this marriage scheme of his. It suggested she held more power over him than he'd ever wanted any woman to have.

The obvious answer to that was to seduce her quickly and sate this hunger that had been building in him since the first instant he'd laid eyes on her again. He was widely regarded as being incredibly persuasive, a talented negotiator. Surely he could talk one normally sweet-tempered, affectionate woman into his arms. He knew she was attracted to him. The kind of passion they'd once shared couldn't possibly die, even from lack of nurturing. There were times even now when he caught her looking at him with a hint of blazing desire in her eyes.

So, he decided, it was all a matter of getting around her mule-headed decision to get even with him for proposing a marriage of convenience in the first place. A few dozen roses, a couple of boxes of expensive chocolates interspersed with several well-timed, bone-melting kisses, and she'd abandon this crazy stance she'd taken. If he couldn't pull it off in Atlanta—and the odds were definitely against that at the moment, he conceded with some regret—then he would just have to wait until they got home.

At his request Mrs. Jeffers was already surreptitiously interviewing prospective new tenants for the boarding house. Surely she would find someone suitable by the first of the week, when he and Katie returned home. And then, because there would be no way to avoid it without revealing to everyone that their marriage was a sham, Katie would have to welcome him into her bedroom.

It was a sneaky, underhanded thing to do, Luke admitted to himself. But every once in a while the end did justify the means. He regarded Katie worriedly and wondered if she would agree. He'd have to ask her. After they'd made love a couple of hundred times seemed like the best timing. If he asked her anytime soon, he doubted if her response would be all that encouraging.

"Katie," he called as he turned into the secluded hotel driveway. When she didn't stir, he caressed her cheek. "Hey, Sleeping Beauty, wake up. We're here."

She blinked sleepily once, twice, then stared at him as alertly as if she'd never nodded off. Her ability to come wide awake in an instant was an admirable trait for the most part. He couldn't help imagining, though, what it would be like to have her awaken in his arms, all sleepily sensual and willing.

His imagination was very vivid. His body was aroused in less time than it took her to peel off her seat belt. While he wondered if he'd even be able to move, she was already smiling brightly at the hotel doorman, who'd just swept open her door.

"Mrs. Cassidy, welcome."

Luke caught Katie's startled expression and was glad he'd at least had the good sense to call ahead and warn the hotel that he was returning with his new bride. He'd stayed there for several weeks while he and Betty Sue had been finalizing their divorce settlement. Just about everyone on the hotel's small, discreet staff knew him well.

"Good evening, Raymond," he called out to the doorman, when he was finally able to step from the car.

"It's good to see you again, sir," he said, handing Luke the suite's key. "I'll have your bags sent directly up."

"Whatever happened to check-in?" Katie inquired dryly as they were whisked to the penthouse floor in a private elevator. "And exactly why are you so well-known here?"

"I lived here for a while."

"And tipped generously, no doubt."

He nodded agreement. "It always pays to reward excellent service."

Katie murmured something he couldn't quite hear.

"What was that?"

"I said for ten thousand, you must be expecting really extraordinary service from me," she said, her chin lifting with a touch of familiar defiance. Glittering green eyes challenged him. "You probably should have tried my cooking, at least, before we got to this point. My fried chicken is good, but I'm not sure it's *that* good."

"Katie..." Luke began, then cut off his protest. What could he say to convince her that she was hardly in the same league as the hotel staff? Or that he didn't give two hoots about her fried chicken? He could readily see how a case could be made that he had bought her services just as impartially as he might those of a maid or a concierge.

He fell into a brooding silence that lasted until he saw her awestruck expression as the elevator door opened into the elegant penthouse with its sweeping view of exquisitely landscaped gardens and city lights. Apparently this much at least he'd done right.

"Oh, my," she murmured.

"Like it?"

The last of her harsh facade dropped away. "It's amazing. I feel as if I'm in someone's very expensive, very tasteful apartment, not a hotel at all." She glanced around slowly. "Except for the basket of fruit and the bottle of champagne. Those are definitely hotel touches."

Since her mood seemed to have shifted, Luke risked taking her hand in his and drawing her over to the windows. He could see her increasingly delighted expression reflected in the glass as she stared out at their surroundings.

Softly lit fountains cascaded amid the well-tended displays of flowers. Romantic pathways wound through the grounds with benches scattered in secluded nooks for private conversations and stolen kisses. He recalled how many times he'd observed couples on those pathways and had felt a shaft of pure envy for the closeness they shared.

Once, long ago, he'd had that kind of uncomplicated intimacy with someone, but he'd thrown it away. His hand around hers tightened instinctively, and at once her expression turned guarded. She tugged her hand free in a deliberate gesture he couldn't mistake.

"Katie..."

"It really is wonderful," she said interrupting, her voice coolly polite.

"The food is excellent. I've ordered dinner. It should be here soon."

"I'm not hungry."

"Katie, you're always hungry."

She shook her head. "Not tonight," she insisted stubbornly. She regarded him speculatively. "You stayed here for a while? How long?"

"Several weeks. I wasn't in this room, but in one very similar on the floor below. Robby stayed at home with his mother until we'd worked out the divorce and custody arrangements."

She regarded him with amazement. "Just how rich are you?"

"Rich enough, I suppose."

"You had all this and you still came back to Clover. Why?"

Luke wasn't prepared to reveal that she had drawn him back, that he'd been consumed by memories of what they'd once shared, that he'd needed something desperately—a mother for Robby—and she'd been the first person who came into his head. Duty to his son and an aching yearning that was his alone had become so intertwined he hadn't been able to separate them.

"I wanted the sort of life that's possible there for Robby," he said instead. "I want him to grow up surrounded by people who will care about him as much as I do. I don't want him to grow up afraid of going to school because of guns the other kids might have. The only sort of gang I want him involved with is a bunch of kids walking to the movies on Saturday night."

"Those are the things you wanted for your son," she said pointedly. "What about for you? What did coming home represent to you?"

He said the first thing that popped into his head. "Peace of mind. I wanted my life back the way it used to be."

Katie seemed surprised by the answer. "Luke, you always hated Clover, hated the small-town mentality. You couldn't wait to get out."

He shrugged. "Hey, darlin', I never said I was perfect. But I did learn from my mistakes, and a longing for urban life was one of them. Just read the headlines. City living these days isn't all it's cracked up to be."

The worst mistake of all, though, had been leaving Katie behind. He'd finally accepted that and come home to claim her, albeit on terms far different from those he'd once imagined. He doubted he could ever love anyone, not even Katie, as freely as he once had. He had no one to blame but himself for the shallowness of his first marriage, but the experience had soured him on the institution and on the kind of love that was supposed to be its foundation.

But surely he and Katie could build a new relationship that would be mutually satisfying without endangering the protective wall he'd erected around his emotions after Betty Sue had left them battered and bruised.

Best friends always understood, were always quick to defend. Best friends never made unreasonable demands. And they never, ever cheated. He thought perhaps that level of loyalty, always granted him by

Katie without hesitation, was something he'd missed most of all in the cutthroat environment in which he'd found himself in Atlanta—at home and in business.

He caught the softening in Katie's expression, and for one brief instant he was able to convince himself that everything was going to be just fine. He circled her waist from behind and stood gazing out over her head. Already a deep sense of peace was stealing through him.

That and desire, he conceded ruefully when the evidence became unmistakable. Katie's sharply indrawn breath hinted that she was aware of it, as well, but she didn't protest, didn't pull away.

Because the moment was so fragile, so fraught with possibilities for doing the wrong thing, Luke did nothing. He just held Katie, her back tucked against his chest, her bottom brushing against his arousal, and thanked his lucky stars that they had come this far. Tomorrow would be soon enough to worry about the rest.

When the lavish dinner Luke had ordered arrived, accompanied by champagne, Katie fled. She could no longer keep up the dangerous charade without fear of getting too caught up in the seductive fantasy it promised.

She quietly, but emphatically shut the door to the hotel suite's bedroom, then leaned against it and sucked in a deep breath. Talk about close calls! She had very nearly succumbed to Luke's unspoken hunger.

Surrounded by his masculine scent, enveloped by his heat, tempted by his hard body, she had felt her already flimsy resolve wavering. It would have been so easy, so natural to give in to the desire that had swept through her at his first touch. And the expensive, intoxicating champagne would have made that capitulation a certainty.

How many nights had she lain awake remembering the way it felt to be held by him? How many months had she imagined the sweet torment of his touches? How many years now had she tried to forget those very same things, only to have the memories reawakened in a heartbeat?

Slowly, she stripped off the pink silk dress she'd worn for her wedding day, then the daring gossamer lace underwear. She reached for the sexy nightie that Lucy had insisted she pack, then went into the huge tiled bathroom and turned on the shower. When the room had filled with steam, she stepped into the marbled enclosure and let the hot water slide over her body, touching her in all the places she had dreamed that Luke would caress tonight. Before she knew it her body was sensitive and throbbing with need.

Groaning, she flipped off the hot water and let the cold water cascade over her until she was shivering and no longer caught up in the kind of desperate yearnings that only Luke could fulfill. The irony, of course, was that tonight he was within reach, only a few feet away, with an unlocked door between them. Legalities and proximity had made him hers, and yet, she couldn't bring herself to claim him.

Stepping out of the shower and putting on the sheer nightie that skimmed her figure, concealing virtually nothing, Katie looked at that door longingly. What was being accomplished by keeping Luke out of her bed? Was she merely trying to salvage her pride?

Or did she hope that the burning desire she'd seen in his eyes would come to translate into love, if only she gave it enough time?

Whatever her eventual goal, the only certainty was that she was about to spend a very sleepless wedding night and for none of the usual, provocative reasons.

"Katie?"

Luke's low voice sent a shaft of pure need through her. "Yes."

"Good night," he called softly.

"Good night," she whispered, as tears brimmed over and spilled down her cheeks. Then lower still, in a voice she knew wouldn't carry through the thick hotel door, she murmured, "Good night, my love."

Chapter Five

The first thing Katie heard when she awoke after a restless night of tossing and turning was the murmur of Luke's voice coming from the living room of their suite. She rolled over and closed her eyes, thinking what a pleasure it was simply to know he was close by. This, she supposed, was one of the little-discussed benefits of marriage, a tiny intimacy that couples grew used to and took for granted. After being separated from him for what seemed an eternity, she doubted she would ever take Luke's presence for granted.

Hearing his low murmur from just behind the closed door was such a unique and wonderful experience that she very well might have stayed in bed and listened to him for hours, except she was starved. Apparently her stomach had suffered nearly as much as her libido with last night's stubborn decision to turn down the wedding supper Luke had ordered—and whatever might have come later.

Hopping out of the luxurious, albeit very lonely bed, she stretched lazily, donned her sexiest bra and panties, then tugged on tan linen slacks, a peach silk blouse, and slipped on a pair of flats. All were new and far dressier than what she usually wore in Clover. Studying herself in the mirror, she decided she could hold her own in the big city.

After a cursory brushing of teeth and hair, she skimmed a pale peach lipstick across her lips, then opened the door into the living room.

Luke was still on the phone. At the sight of her, he murmured a hurried goodbye, then hung up, a slow smile spreading across his face, transforming his too-serious expression into a look that was pure invitation.

Katie's composure suddenly slipped. Luke was wearing a pair of dress slacks, zipped up, but unbuttoned at the waist, and nothing else. His hair was curling damply. His chest was...well, his chest didn't bear too close an examination. Her heart was thumping hard enough as it was. If he'd stripped down this provocatively last night instead of offering far less intoxicating champagne, she never would have made it to that huge bed alone. Determined not to let the tantalizing effect ruin her stance this morning, she reminded herself that he, at least, was in Atlanta for the sole purpose of conducting business, not seduction.

Or so he claimed. The current dangerous gleam in his eyes suggested otherwise.

"Hard at work already, I see," she said when she thought she could get the words out without giving her susceptibility away by sounding too breathless.

"Ordering breakfast, actually," he countered with another of those smiles that could have melted an Arctic iceberg. "I hope you still love pancakes, scrambled eggs, bacon, strawberries and fresh-squeezed orange juice."

"I do, but all at once?"

"It's a special occasion."

"What are we celebrating?" she inquired innocently. "Did a big deal go through?"

That high-voltage smile dissipated. He scowled at her. "Okay, Katie, enough with the sarcasm. You made your point last night. Turning our honeymoon into a business trip was a rotten idea."

She nodded with satisfaction. "It's nice to see you grasp things so readily. No wonder you're wildly successful in business."

"However," he said, as if she hadn't spoken. "If you want a real honeymoon, then it can't be one-sided on my part. You have to cooperate."

Her gaze narrowed as she considered the suspicious glint in his eyes and the dare in his voice. "Cooperate?"

"No shopping with old Cee-Cee and Pris."

"But I was really looking forward to it," she protested just to taunt him.

"About as much as a flu shot," he muttered.

"I don't take flu shots."

"My point exactly."

Katie began to get the notion that she'd won the first round in this latest test of wills. The taste of victory was definitely sweet. She relented and grinned at him. "Okay, no business for you. No shopping for me. What'll we do?" Having three whole days stretched out ahead of them seemed to offer limitless, very intriguing possibilities.

"There are certain traditional things a bride and groom usually do on a honeymoon," he suggested hopefully.

"You wish," she countered. "How about sight-seeing?"

"Sight-seeing?" he repeated blankly as if the concept were totally foreign.

"You lived here six years. Surely you know all the most fascinating local sights. I want to see them."

"Actually, about the only thing I ever saw was the downtown skyscraper where my office was located."

His revelation was hardly surprising. Luke's single-mindedness was exactly the trait that had made him a success. Katie remained undaunted. "We'll buy a guidebook." She paused thoughtfully. "And a map."

"I can get around. We don't need a map."

"Luke, you used to get lost in Clover."

He frowned at the teasing comment. "I did not."

"What about the time we were supposed to go to Mindy Prescott's birthday party and we got there an hour late because you refused to stop and ask directions?"

"She didn't live in Clover," he said defensively. "And those country roads weren't marked. That map she drew was a joke. Whoever heard of telling someone that a house is just past the first big curve in the highway, a half mile beyond the big oak on the left and right after a dilapidated red barn?''

''Just because you couldn't tell an oak from a maple if your life depended on it, don't go blaming Mindy Prescott,'' Katie retorted. ''We were halfway to Charleston before you finally gave in and let me call to ask where we'd gone wrong. Wandering around lost must be some macho, male thing.''

He gave her a rueful grin. ''Okay, we'll buy a map. Satisfied?''

About the map, definitely, Katie thought. Her body, however, was protesting vehemently. She wanted food and she wanted Luke, not necessarily in that order. Her gaze met his and something of her longing must have been in her eyes, because he suddenly went perfectly still. Electricity arced between them. The air practically crackled with it. Katie's defenses wobbled dangerously.

''Katie,'' he said softly, the lure in his voice almost irresistible.

''Luke,'' she whispered, suddenly trembling with all of the sensual anticipation she'd been fighting to keep at bay.

Their gazes locked. But before either of them could take the first, fateful step to close the space between them, the suite's doorbell chimed loudly. The sound echoed through the room, breaking the fragile moment.

As if that weren't enough disruption, the phone started ringing.

Katie viewed Luke with some regret—and admittedly a certain amount of relief. It was far too soon to allow all of those protective barriers she'd erected to be torn down, and there wasn't a doubt in her mind that they'd been about to topple. This was just further proof that she had about as much natural resistance to Luke as a badly constructed roof did to a hurricane.

"You get the phone. I'll get the door," she suggested briskly.

"Let's ignore them both," he countered, his gaze never leaving her face.

She searched his expression for evidence of sincerity. "If I agreed, would you really be able to stand not knowing who's on the phone?"

He sighed. "Unfortunately I have a very good idea who it is. My secretary. I spoke to her earlier."

"When? Before dawn on a Sunday morning?" she inquired, glancing at her watch.

"She makes herself available whenever I need her."

"I'll bet," Katie muttered.

Luke regarded her with amusement. "Jealous?"

"Hardly."

"Then you won't mind if I grab this. She's supposed to be rescheduling my business meetings for another time."

"Then by all means, talk to her," Katie said as she went to the door to admit the waiter with their breakfast order.

As she chatted with the waiter—or tried to—she heard snatches of Luke's terse phone conversation. His previously lighthearted mood had given way to an unmistakable anger that was evident not just in his tone of voice, but in his tense shoulders and sudden pacing.

"No, absolutely not," he snapped, then lowered his voice to say something that Katie couldn't hear.

The waiter, to his credit, never even looked away from the service cart, which he had pushed into a nook overlooking the gardens. He finished removing the silver tops from the serving dishes, then discreetly left them alone without any hint that he'd overheard Luke's display of temper or that he'd noticed the pile of blankets on the honeymoon suite sofa.

At first, after the waiter had gone, Katie was too caught up in sampling the strawberries and the light, fluffy pancakes to notice Luke's increasingly murderous expression or to pay much attention to his tersely-worded conversation. She assumed it had something to do with a business deal gone awry. When his sharply raised voice suddenly caught her attention, she paused with her fork halfway to her mouth.

"No, dammit! I don't want you anywhere near Clover and that's final," he said and slammed down the phone with a force that shook the delicate mahogany table on which it was sitting.

Katie regarded him worriedly. She was certain she had never seen Luke so furious. No matter how far he'd ever been pushed—by circumstances or by Tommy or by her, for that matter—he'd never exploded like this. She watched as he visibly tried to compose himself before turning and walking toward her.

"Luke, what on earth was that about?"

"It's nothing for you to worry about," he said. "How's the food?"

Katie frowned at the dismissal. "The food is fine. You're obviously not. Was that your secretary? Did some business deal fall apart?"

"Not everything in my life has to do with business," he snapped.

"Okay, then," she said, clinging to her patience by a thread. She recalled his mentioning Clover and tried to guess what that had to do with anything. "Has something happened at home? Is Robby okay?"

"I'm sure Robby's fine," he said, his voice suspiciously tight. "Everything's fine."

She didn't believe him for a minute. "If business is fine and Robby is fine, then what's wrong?" she prodded, determined to make him open up. "It's obvious you're still seething about something."

"It was nothing," he contradicted heatedly. "I'll deal with it."

Katie flinched at his determination to shut her out. That fragile thread on her patience snapped. "Well, pardon me for wanting to help. I guess I don't have this marriage business down quite yet. Our deal must not have included common courtesy."

Luke's reaction to her sarcasm was immediate and apologetic. "I'm sorry, Katie."

She regarded him doubtfully.

"I am," he insisted. "I guess I don't have it down just yet either."

Because he looked so miserable and distraught, Katie waited until her own temper had cooled before she spoke. "Luke, this is new to both of us. I don't have all the answers, but I do know one thing. It won't work if we don't learn to share what's going on in our lives. If there's some business crisis or something, I may not be able to help you solve it, but I can always listen. You know that. You used to talk to me about everything."

For an instant he seemed to be wavering. She thought for sure he was going to open up, to tell her what had ruined his mood so thoroughly, but then his jaw tightened and he shook his head. "This isn't the time to get into it."

"It? What is it?" she asked in exasperation.

He threw down his napkin and got up from the table. "Not now, Katie." He grabbed a shirt from the back of the chair and tugged it on. He was still buttoning it as he headed for the door. "I'll be back."

With a sinking sensation in the pit of her stomach, she watched him open the door. She sensed that if he walked out now, it would establish a pattern from which they might never recover. "Luke, don't go. Please."

He turned then and gave her a halfhearted ghost of a smile. "Don't worry. I won't be gone long."

He shut the door before she could protest that running out, when they should be talking, might well have worse consequences than whatever problem he had on his mind.

Damn Tommy for ruining the morning for him, Luke thought as he walked the hotel grounds in a futile attempt to calm down. Tommy's timing couldn't have been worse. Luke had sensed that he and Katie were finally getting closer just before the phone had rung. Now that he'd clearly withheld information from her, they were further apart than ever. He couldn't blame her for being furious.

At the moment, though, she was no more furious than he was, albeit for far different reasons. How typical of Tommy to wait until he was off on his honeymoon before calling and making more threats. When Tommy had said he was going to Clover to visit Robby while Luke was away, a fierce tide of anger had rolled through him. It was yet more proof that Tommy didn't give a damn about his son's feelings. He was only using the boy to taunt Luke, hoping for a big cash settlement, no doubt, in return for backing off.

Luke couldn't help wondering if his vehement protest would be enough to keep his brother away. He doubted it. Tommy had never listened to a damn thing he had to say. There was no reason to believe that that had changed. The only difference now was that the stakes were higher than they had been when they were kids.

The thought of his brother being alone with Robby sent chills through him. Tommy would never physically harm the boy. Luke was certain of that. But he would start filling Robby's head with whatever garbage suited his purposes. He wouldn't worry a bit about whatever psychological damage he might be doing in the process. It would never cross Tommy's selfish mind that revealing the truth to Robby might be devastating.

Luke suddenly knew he couldn't risk that happening. He had to call Peg at once and warn her to keep

Tommy away from Robby. She would want to know why. There was no getting around that. If he expected her cooperation, he would have to tell her the truth, all of it.

At the prospect of revealing everything to Katie's aunt, he shuddered. Peg would have his hide for this, especially if she found out he had told Katie none of it.

"Damn," he muttered. It was all unraveling. He'd wanted time. Time to prepare Katie. Time for her to start thinking of Robby as her own. Time for her to become committed to being both wife and mother.

Now it seemed that his time had run out. He had to tell Katie everything. He had to let her know the fight they were in for. She had to be prepared for the bitterness and ugly accusations that were likely to come with the custody dispute.

But now? On their honeymoon? Surely it would be wrong to spoil these few days. He resolved to tell her the moment they returned to Clover. In the meantime, he knew he could count on Peg's discretion. More, he knew he could count on her to protect Robby.

The decision made, he stopped by a pay phone in the hotel lobby and called Peg's Diner. When Peg picked up, he didn't mince words. His voice tight, he just outlined the situation, then extracted her promise to keep Tommy away from his son.

"Of course, I'll see to it that he's not alone with Robby for a minute," she said readily. "I haven't seen any sign of him around town. Maybe he won't show up at all."

"He'll show up," Luke said with certainty. Knowing that, he realized what he had to do. "I think maybe Katie and I ought to get back there. We can be home by this afternoon."

Peg fell silent at that. He could practically feel her disapproval crackling over the phone line.

"Peg, it's the only way," he insisted. "I can't leave you to stand up to Tommy. This mess isn't your responsibility."

"Luke, that brother of yours doesn't scare me. He never did. It does worry me, though, that you and Katie are starting off your marriage by facing such a big problem. You need a few days by yourselves to build up the strength this fight is going to take. Stop fussing about the burden you're placing on me and think about your marriage. Let these few days alone be my wedding gift to the two of you."

Luke sighed. "Peg, I know you mean well and there's no one I'd trust more with my son, but—"

"No 'buts.' You two stay and enjoy yourselves. I'll see you on Wednesday, just the way we planned. If anything comes up I can't handle, I'll call you immediately. If I have to, I'll get Ford Maguire to set Tommy straight."

As much as he liked Ford, Luke wasn't sure he wanted the sheriff mixed up in this. "I'll think about it," he said eventually. "Is Robby there? I'd like to speak to him."

"He's sitting in one of the booths with his coloring books. I've got an order in for his breakfast now. Hang on, I'll get him for you."

Luke could hear Robby's whoop of excitement when Peg told him who was on the phone. For the first time since Tommy's call, he smiled.

"Daddy, is it really you?"

"It's me, my man. How are you doing? Are you and Peg having fun?"

"She rented a movie for me last night and she made pizza. Did you know you could make it at home?"

"So I've heard," Luke said, thinking of the times they'd ordered it in Atlanta. They'd had most of their dinners delivered the same way. No wonder Robby sounded so stunned by the concept of homemade pizza. He'd probably never guessed what the oven was for before. "How was it?"

"The best. She put pepperoni on it and everything."

"That's great, pal. What movie did you see?"

"*Flintstones*. Remember when we saw that? Mommy hated it."

Actually, Betty Sue had hated most anything with a G rating, as Luke recalled. Her whole blasted life-style would have been X-rated by the movie industry. It really was too bad Tommy hadn't stuck around. They were a perfect pair.

But then he wouldn't have had Robby, Luke reminded himself. "I miss you, pal," he said softly, an unexpected catch in his voice.

"Miss you," Robby echoed. "I gotta go. Aunt Peg just brought me pancakes. And Mrs. Jeffers said she'd take me to ride my bike as soon as I eat. And tomorrow Aunt Peg and me are going to the beach. It's her day off."

"Sounds like you have a busy time planned."

"Hey, Daddy?"

"Yes."

"I really, really like it here."

Luke closed his eyes and sucked in a deep breath. It was turning out just the way he'd envisioned. He was finally giving Robby the real home he deserved, complete with a loving extended family. "I'm glad, pal. Really, really glad."

When he'd hung up, Luke vowed silently that he would destroy Tommy if he did anything, anything at all to ruin Robby's new-found happiness.

Katie took one look at Luke's face when he finally came back to the suite, and all of her pent-up anger died at once. His face looked haggard and his shoulders were slumped, as if he carried the weight of the world on them.

Instead of verbally hurling the accusations and prying questions she'd formulated in her head, she poured him a cup of coffee and said mildly, "I saved some pancakes and fruit for you. You look like you could use them."

He accepted the cup of coffee and ignored the rest. He walked directly to the window and stood staring down at the gardens, his expression troubled.

Katie plunged on, trying to sound as if everything were perfectly normal. "Your secretary called. She said she was able to reschedule everything for the first week in July."

"That's good," he said with a distracted air.

"I'm thinking of having my hair dyed purple while we're here," she said.

"If that's what you want."

"Luke!"

His head snapped around. "What?"

Katie regarded him with dismay. "Talk about it," she ordered.

He didn't pretend not to know what *it* was. "Later."

"When?"

"Just later. Let it go, Katie."

She sighed and gave up. Years of experience should have taught her that she couldn't badger Luke into talking before he was ready. "So, what do you want to do today?"

He drew in a deep, shuddering breath before finally facing her. "I want to go home."

The last of her illusions that they could salvage this honeymoon dissolved. "You want to go home?" she repeated with dismay. "Today?"

He nodded. "I'll make it up to you. I promise."

"You've been making a lot of promises to me recently," Katie said, struggling to keep her voice even, trying even harder not to cry. "Any idea when you'll start keeping a few of them?"

Stormy blue eyes met hers. "As soon as we're home, we'll sit down and I'll explain everything."

Judging from Luke's bleak expression, Katie had an awful feeling that she wasn't going to like the explanation a bit. "Why do I have this terrible hunch that it's coming about twenty-four hours too late?"

Chapter Six

The second call to Peg Jones to let her know that he and Katie would definitely be returning to Clover had been a terrible mistake, Luke realized as they drove toward the boarding house. A collection of cars stretched for blocks in every direction. He doubted that one of the boarders had invited half the town to drop by.

More likely, the warning he had given Peg had allowed her just enough time to prepare the full-blown wedding reception she'd wanted for the two of them in the first place. He should have known that small gathering at her house the day before wouldn't satisfy her. Or maybe she was just retaliating for what she considered to be his ill-advised decision to cut the honeymoon short.

"What do you suppose...?" Katie began, then turned to Luke with a horrified expression on her face. "Oh, no, surely she didn't."

"Oh, I think it's a safe bet that we are about to be congratulated by everyone in Clover," Luke said grimly. He glanced at Katie's pale face and immediately took pity on her. "We could hide out at the hotel."

"That would be cowardly," she said, but she turned a wistful look on the two-story building that was visible a few blocks away.

"I prefer to think of it as a strategic retreat."

Katie buried her face in her hands. "What are they going to think? We've been married barely over a day and we cut short our honeymoon."

Luke honestly hadn't considered the likelihood of embarrassing Katie when he'd made the impulsive decision to come back to Clover early. He'd been focused entirely on preventing a meeting between his brother and Robby.

"I'm sorry. I wasn't thinking of how this might look." He reached for her hand, which was ice-cold. Impulsively, he brushed a kiss across her knuckles. "I'm serious, we can turn right around and stay at a motel out on the highway. We don't even have to stay at the hotel here in town."

"That's a little like closing the barn door after the horse has gone," she observed dryly. "Obviously everyone already knows we cut the honeymoon short. They've been invited here to celebrate our return."

"Maybe they'll just think Peg got it wrong."

"Yeah, right," she said in a voice laden with skepticism. "Peg has been taking orders at the diner for thirty years without making a note. She's never made a mistake. Do you honestly think anyone will believe she made a little error about something as important as our scheduled return from our honeymoon?" She shook her head. "No way. We're just going to have to brazen it out."

Filled with self-loathing for having put her in this position, Luke regarded her worriedly. "Can you do that?"

Katie's chin rose a determined notch. "I'll have to, won't I?" She turned to him, eyes suddenly blazing with fury. "But when this little charade ends, Luke Cassidy, you'd better have some damned good answers ready or this could well be the shortest marriage on record in the entire state of South Carolina. In fact, I might very well go for an annulment."

Apparently assured that Luke understood the implication of that threat, she flung open the car door and exited with the regal demeanor of a queen going to greet her subjects. Luke was left to trail along in her wake and wonder if she would make good on the threat. He decided he'd better do something damned quick to better the odds against it. Tommy would have a heyday in court with news that his brief marriage had been annulled because it had never been consummated, to say nothing of the blow it would be to Luke's ego to have the information bandied about.

Just outside the door he captured Katie's elbow and brought her to a halt. There was only one way he knew to keep Katie from blowing their charade, only one way he'd ever known to silence her—by kissing her senseless. Though he'd refrained from using the tactic thus far, he wasn't above hauling it out whenever it suited his purposes. It most definitely suited him now.

"Let's make it look good, darlin'," he said.

Before she could offer a protest, he scooped her into his arms for the traditional trip across the threshold. While he was at it, he planted a slow, lingering kiss on lips that clearly had been about to shout a vehement protest. He suspected that only the fact that a cheer had gone up at the sight of their entrance kept Katie from landing her fist squarely against his nose.

Luke discovered he rather liked holding Katie captive. It was the first moment since this entire debacle had begun that he truly felt like a newlywed. He sure as hell hadn't felt like one while he'd been trying to sleep—alone—on that cramped sofa the night before. He decided he might as well take advantage of the moment and steal another kiss that Katie would otherwise deny him. No doubt he would pay for it later, but the way his pulse was bucking told him it would be worth the cost.

As he shifted her in his arms to lower her slowly to her feet, he made very sure that Katie slid down his body until every square inch of him blazed as if it had been touched by the summer sun.

When she would have made a dash for it, he cupped her cheeks in his hands and held her face perfectly still. Katie's eyes widened as she watched him warily. Her lips parted, probably to form another vehement protest. But Luke swooped in to steal the words, sealing his mouth over hers, savoring the sweet taste.

Katie's entire body tensed for the space of a heartbeat, but if there was one thing Luke knew it was the nuances of a kiss. From that first possessive claiming, his lips turned gentle, persuasive.

The coaxing worked. He knew the precise instant when Katie stopped fighting him and became an enthusiastic participant. Her skin heated. Her pulse skittered wildly. Her tongue tentatively sought out his.

From gentle persuasion, the kiss quickly escalated into a dark, moist, mysterious invitation that had his blood roaring through his veins. Suddenly he wanted Katie upstairs, in his bed, under him. He wanted it with a desperation that stunned him.

Staggered by this unexpected need to claim her, Luke forgot all about where they were and how the game had started. A single whoop of approval, echoed by a half dozen more, and punctuated by applause, snapped him back to an unfortunate reality. He and Katie were definitely not alone. From the dazed look in her eyes, she was no happier about that discovery than he was.

All too quickly, though, their true circumstances took the blush out of her cheeks and made her eyes blaze not with passion, but with fury. Luke knew with certainty that he would hear about this when they were alone. Worse, he suspected that would be just the beginning of what Katie had to say, none of it pleasant.

"Later," he whispered in a determinedly seductive purr he hoped would remind her of the provocative intimacy they'd just shared.

"You'd better believe it," she said tightly.

Katie might have been thinking about that bone-melting kiss, but Luke doubted it. Her tone was more in keeping with a deadly courtroom cross-examination.

Before he could try to defuse her temper, Peg swooped in to hug Katie, and Robby rushed up to hurl himself into Luke's arms. Within seconds Robby was racing off with another boy about his own age. Luke stared after them with amusement. He realized with a start how rarely he'd seen his child playing with friends. It was yet another confirmation that coming back to Clover had been the right decision.

By the time Luke glanced around, Katie was surrounded by her friends, most of whom had barely a word to spare for him, though he'd known them all his life. He hadn't thought it possible in a town where he'd grown up, but apparently six years away had made him an outsider. And if the scowl on Lucy Ryder's face was an indication, at the moment she wished he'd stayed in Atlanta forever.

Maybe people just had long memories, he speculated. Maybe they remembered with absolute clarity that he and Katie had been best friends. Maybe they suspected how far things had gone before he'd walked out on her. And maybe they resented being left behind to deal with the aftermath of his lousy treatment of a woman they all adored.

Whatever it was, everyone welcomed Katie home as if she'd been off on a safari for months, rather than an abbreviated one-day honeymoon. Peg, in particular, surveyed her niece as if looking for signs that Luke had done anything, anything at all to make her miserable. Katie's bright smile and glowing cheeks—the products of determination and makeup—apparently convinced her all was well.

Katie, whom he would have sworn didn't have a shred of artifice in her, turned out to have superb acting skills. Not a single person in the room—with the possible exception of Lucy—would have guessed from her cheerful demeanor that their marriage was an unconsummated farce. Only he seemed to notice the tiny lines of strain around her mouth, the faint shadows under her eyes, the forced note of her laughter, the way she fiddled nervously with a strand of hair.

For three hours he accepted cursory congratulations on winning the prettiest woman in town, he endured less-than-subtle winks about the honeymoon, and took advice from half the women in town on how to keep his new bride happy and content. Hannah, Sophie and Emma had some very intriguing ideas for the future bliss of the woman who'd been their bridesmaid.

Through it all he kept his gaze pinned on Katie, wondering exactly when she would break, worrying whether be would be able to clear out the guests before it happened. He was still worried about that when Peg cornered him.

"I'm keeping Robby at my place a few more nights," she informed him in a tone that invited no argument. Facing him defiantly, she added, "I've also arranged for the boarders to go to the hotel for the rest of the week. I can understand your feeling a need to be in Clover in case your brother decides to make good on his threat, but I will not allow you to spoil my niece's honeymoon.''

Luke didn't have the heart to tell her that Katie was probably thrilled to be back among friends or that the last thing Peg's niece wanted was to be left alone with him. And, given the dire looks Katie had been directing at him for the past couple of hours, he wasn't so sure he wanted to be left alone with her.

''I'll pay for the rooms at the hotel,'' he volunteered since it seemed unlikely that anyone was going to go contrary to Peg's plans.

''That's what I told them,'' Peg said dryly.

He grinned at her. ''You think of everything.''

''I do try,'' she said cheerfully. ''How did Katie take the news about the custody battle?''

Luke swallowed hard and admitted, ''I haven't told her yet.''

Muttering something that sounded suspiciously unladylike under her breath, Peg latched on to his elbow and dragged him into the kitchen. ''Luke Cassidy, what in tarnation were you thinking of? She has a right to know. Does she have any idea at all what brought you back here in such an all-fired hurry?''

''Not exactly.''

''So for all she knows, you just got tired of being alone with her,'' she snapped.

''Of course not,'' he said, but knew it was possible that that was exactly what Katie thought.

Peg clearly didn't buy the denial any more than he did. She regarded him as if he were slightly lower than pond scum. ''I swear if you don't tell her everything by tomorrow morning, then I will. I can't begin to imagine what she must be thinking. Wasn't it bad enough that you walked out on her once before? Ripped the hell out of her self-esteem, you did. Now you've got her thinking you don't even want to spend three days alone with her. My glory, why'd you even bother asking her to marry you?''

Luke was very much afraid if Peg had too long to think about that question, she'd hit the answer square on the head. "As soon as everyone is out of here and we have the place to ourselves, I'll tell her everything.''

"See that you do," Peg ordered, her voice tight. "Just to speed things up, I'll start clearing these folks out. Don't worry about the mess. I have someone coming in to clean up first thing in the morning.''

Luke couldn't imagine Katie being patient enough to leave the dirty dishes scattered around the house. While Peg hustled everyone toward the door, he began picking up, carting trays of glasses and dessert plates into the kitchen and loading them into the industrial-size dishwasher that looked like a relic from the early days of Peg's Diner.

He'd just hauled a sack of trash to the garbage cans out back, when he looked up and spotted Katie waiting for him in the kitchen door. For one fleeting instant, he imagined that they were a typical couple, tired but elated after a night of entertaining. He could almost envision the two of them settling on the sofa side by side to nibble on leftovers, share bits of gossip, maybe even steal few sweet kisses tasting of wine. It was an image that had once filled his dreams back in the days when he'd had his entire life planned out and Katie had been at the center of it.

But as he neared the back door, one quick survey of Katie's expression told him there would be nothing sweet or simple about the next couple of hours. She clearly hadn't forgotten for one single minute her determination to get the answers that he'd been unwilling to provide earlier.

"There's a nice breeze," he observed, hoping to distract her. "Want to sit in the hammock for a while?"

She glared at him. "No, I do not want to sit in the hammock. We need to talk."

"Those two things aren't mutually exclusive. Last I heard we could talk in the hammock."

"But we won't and you know it," she said flatly.

Luke grinned. "I see you remember that old hammock Peg had in the backyard and the use we put it to."

She sighed. "I remember a lot of things, Luke Cassidy, including the fact that you've been hiding something important from me."

"That wasn't exactly what I was trying to get you to recall."

"I'm sure. Come on, Cassidy. Stop dawdling. It's time to face the music."

Luke sighed as he trudged up the back steps with Katie watching him every step of the way, probably to make sure he didn't take off. In the doorway, he could easily have walked around her, but he made sure he squeezed past, brushing tantalizingly against breasts and thighs just enough to stir his own senses, if not hers.

Sure enough, heat flared in her eyes. He seized on that. "You know, Peg went to a lot of trouble to see that we had some time alone here. It would be a shame to waste it, don't you think?"

"What I think is that you're trying to make me forget all the questions I have," she said, frowning at him.

"No doubt about it," he admitted candidly. He grinned unrepentantly.

"Why is that? What are you hiding? And what makes you think a few kisses—"

"Or more," he taunted.

She scowled. "Or anything on God's green earth will make me forget what's on my mind?"

Luke stubbornly resisted being drawn into that discussion. "If I can't distract you with images of all the wild, provocative things we could do in that hammock, let's talk about that big, old featherbed of yours."

"Luke, you could dance around the living room stark naked and I wouldn't forget what's on my mind." She waved an envelope he hadn't noticed before in his face. "Especially since this apparently arrived while we were gone. Any idea what it might be?"

From her tone, he guessed that she knew precisely what was inside that thick envelope.

"A sweepstakes entry?" he suggested.

Katie looked as if she were about to explode. "Dammit, don't you dare try to make a joke out of this," she snapped without any pretense of tolerance.

Luke heaved a sigh. It looked as if they were going to have this discussion whether the time was right or not. "Okay, you're the one who's opened the envelope. Why don't you tell me what's inside."

"Offhand, I'd say they're custody papers," she said, her voice flat. Her gaze swept over him before settling into a challenging glare. "Why the hell would your brother be fighting you for custody of Robby?"

Despite his promise to Peg, Luke really hadn't wanted to get into this tonight. They'd had a long, exhausting, stressful day as it was. He'd hoped when he laid it all out in the morning—before Peg had a chance to do it for him—Katie would be fresh, maybe even receptive. Right now she looked anything but. In fact, she seemed inclined to tar and feather him. He couldn't in all honesty say he blamed her. He reminded himself that he'd invested ten thousand dollars thus far in at least getting her to listen.

"It's a long story," he said wearily.

"As I recall our vows, there was something about till death do us part," she said. "We have time."

Luke winced at her sarcasm. It appeared the honeymoon was over.

Katie's cheeks burned with humiliation as she squared off against her new husband. It appeared she had let Luke make a fool of her not once, but twice. The papers she clutched in her hand proved that he had lied to her. As if his spoken reasons for marrying her hadn't been flimsy enough, now it appeared they were nothing compared to those he'd kept silent. She couldn't even begin to imagine what that whole story was. Why the dickens would Tommy think he had any claim at all to Robby?

"I'm waiting," she said, glaring at Luke.

"Maybe we'd better sit down. This could take a while," Luke said.

With some reluctance, Katie sat, choosing a chair rather than the sofa, to keep Luke from sitting next to her and clouding her ability to reason. The immobilizing effect he had on her brain was what had gotten her into this mess.

"I wanted to tell you," Luke swore, his gaze pleading with her to believe him.

"Why didn't you? Did the cat have your tongue?"

"You said you didn't want to get into anything serious," he reminded her.

"When did I say that?"

"Friday night."

Katie regarded him incredulously. "The night before the wedding? Wasn't that a bit late to be bringing up the little matter of a custody dispute over your son? Don't you think you should have mentioned it, oh, perhaps when you first asked me to marry you?"

"Probably."

"Why didn't you?"

"I was afraid if I got into everything, you'd turn me down."

Katie didn't deny it. She had a gut-deep feeling his fears had probably been justified. "Maybe I'd better hear what *everything* is before I tell you what my response would have been. Come on, Luke. Spit it out. From the beginning."

Luke walked over to the window and stood staring out. "It all started six years ago," he said.

His voice was so low Katie had to strain to hear him. "Six years ago," she repeated just to be certain she had heard correctly.

Luke nodded. "Betty Sue Wilder came to me and told me she was pregnant."

Katie had already guessed that much. As much as it hurt to think that Luke had slept with another woman around the same time he had made love to her, she had accepted that. "So you did the honorable thing," she said.

"It was a little more complicated than that. She wasn't carrying my baby."

She stared at him in open-mouthed astonishment. "I beg your pardon? The baby wasn't yours? Then what did it have to do with you?" she asked, even though she was already beginning to get the picture.

"Tommy is Robby's natural father."

"Tommy is Robby's father," she repeated slowly, realizing even as she said it that she wasn't nearly as surprised as she should have been.

"No," Luke said angrily, turning to face her. "Robby is my son. I'm his father in every way that counts. When Tommy wouldn't accept responsibility for Betty Sue's pregnancy, I stepped in. I was there in the delivery room when he was born. I gave him my name. I've stayed up nights with him when he was sick. I was there for his first step. I took him to his first day of school. Tommy has never even laid eyes on him."

His voice throbbed with barely contained rage. Whatever else might be true, Katie recognized that Luke considered Robby as much his as if he had made Betty Sue pregnant. There could be no disputing the love he felt for his son. She knew from being raised by her aunt that the bonds formed by day-to-day parenting were as powerful as any connection through biology alone.

And now Tommy was threatening that relationship. She could understand Luke's outrage. What she didn't comprehend was why Tommy would wait all this time to stake a claim to his son. Or exactly where she fit into this.

"Why would Tommy turn up to ask for custody after all this time?"

Luke's mouth twisted. "Money, why else?"

"I don't understand."

"He doesn't want Robby, not really. He expects me to pay him off to stay out of Robby's life."

Kate felt sick to her stomach. "Surely you're wrong. Not even Tommy would turn a little boy's life upside down just so he could get a payout from you."

"He doesn't think it will come to that, of course. I'm sure he's convinced I'll settle with him to keep Robby from ever finding out the truth."

"Frankly, I'm surprised you haven't," Katie said.

"If I thought that would be the end of it, I might have," Luke admitted. "But it wouldn't. It would be the beginning. Every time Tommy needed cash, he'd be back making his threats again. I want it over with here and now. I want a judge to put an end to it.

Somehow I'll make sure that the truth doesn't hurt Robby.''

It took every bit of strength Katie had left to voice the fear that no amount of rational tap-dancing around it could silence. "Could you lose custody?''

Luke finally met her gaze evenly. "With you in court beside me, there's far less likelihood of that. What judge would take a boy away from a happy, whole family and turn him over to a drifting single father?''

Katie swallowed hard against the bile that rose in her throat. There it was, the whole truth, spelled out plain as day. He'd wanted a wife to take into court. Any woman would have done.

Yet Luke had handpicked her to be his son's mother, not because she was so special, but because he had guessed that she was the one woman on earth who couldn't deny him anything. She was his insurance in court. The last of her illusions about their marriage shattered like so much spun glass.

Worse, she knew that even knowing the whole bitter truth, she couldn't walk away. He'd chosen well. Katie would stay by his side. She would see to it that he didn't lose his son to his ne'er-do-well brother.

And, if there was a God in heaven, Luke would never know what staying cost her.

Chapter Seven

"Katie?"

Luke had to repeat himself twice before she finally looked up. The desolation in her eyes was almost his undoing. If there had been any other solution to his problem, he would have released her from her commitment to him on the spot. Something deep inside told him, however, that if he gave her up now, he would regret it the rest of his life. With circumstances as they were, he could only vow that he would make it up to her someday if only she would stick with him. He hoped that promise would be enough.

Though why she should believe anything he had to say at this point was beyond him.

"Katie," he began again now that he had her attention.

Apparently guessing that he was about to offer more empty words, she cut him off. "Don't worry," she said tersely. "I'm not going to walk away now."

A sigh of relief shuddered through him. "Thank you. I knew I could count on you."

"Good old Katie," she muttered under her breath.

Luke heard the hint of resentment in her voice and regarded her warily. "What was that?"

She shook her head. "Nothing," she said wearily, then added more briskly, "What do we need to do to get ready to fight Tommy?"

"For starters, we have to be sure that no one guesses that this is anything less than a perfect marriage," he said slowly, watching her closely.

"Meaning?"

Her cold, impersonal, matter-of-fact tone worried him. He would almost have preferred to have her shouting at him. This docile acceptance was thoroughly out of character. He felt personally to blame for having drained all of the spirit out of her.

Or perhaps it was simply exhaustion. She had a right to be physically and emotionally tired after what she'd been through. By tomorrow she'd probably be screaming at him at the top of her lungs. Ironically, for once he had a feeling he'd welcome the change in her mood.

In the meantime, though, he recognized that this was definitely not the time to mention that Mrs. Jeffers had found a new boarder whose arrival would necessitate making new sleeping arrangements for him and Robby. He was determined that at least to all outside observers, he and Katie would appear to be typical newlyweds. If they were sharing a room, no one would know for certain what went on behind the closed door. If they weren't in the same bedroom, who knew what people would make of it.

"Maybe we'd better talk about it in the morning," he suggested. "I've given you enough to absorb for one night."

"I think I'd rather get everything out in the open now," she countered in that same flat tone. "Come on, Luke. Lay it all out on the table so I know exactly what I'm up against."

Luke was literally saved by the bell. The front door chime was being punched with a great deal of what he recognized as childish fervor. Robby, no doubt, but what the devil was he doing back here tonight? Torn between gratitude for his timing and panic, Luke jumped up. "I'll get it."

When he opened the door, he wasn't exactly surprised to find Robby and Peg on the threshold. Still, his whole body tensed. He knew it would have taken some sort of major calamity for Peg to intrude on them.

"Well, hi," he said with forced cheer. "I wasn't expecting you two back tonight." He studied Peg's expression for some hint about why they'd returned.

"I had a call from your brother," she explained.

Her tone gave away nothing, but Luke knew at once the call must have shaken her or she would never have come back to the boarding house.

"Really?" he said, his tone just as bland. "What did he want?"

"He said he was planning to arrive in Clover to-night and hoped to see..." she glanced down at Robby, but said "...you. I thought you'd probably want Robby to be with you when he arrives."

"What on earth made him call you?" Luke muttered, though nothing Tommy did should startle him after all these years of seeing his brother's canniness in action.

"Obviously someone here in town is keeping him up-to-date on Robby's whereabouts," Peg replied. "Any idea who that might be?"

Luke shook his head. "I can't imagine who would be in touch with him."

"What about your ex-wife?" Katie said from behind him. "Or her parents?"

Luke had been so absorbed in digesting Peg's news that he hadn't even been aware that Katie had joined them in the foyer.

Robby, who was clutching his favorite fire engine and a ragged teddy bear, seemed to pick up on the adults' tension. "Is Mommy here?" he asked, looking up into Luke's face.

"I don't think so, sport. When you talked to her last week, she was still in Seattle, remember?"

"Oh," Robby said flatly, clearly disappointed, but trying valiantly to hide it.

"Maybe you'd better be getting to bed," Luke told his son. "Why don't I take you up and see that you're settled in?"

"What about..." He hesitated, his sleepy, blue-eyed gaze fixed hopefully on Katie. "I don't know what to call you now that you and Daddy are married."

Luke's breath snagged in his throat as he waited for her response. There was only the faintest pause and a quick glance at Luke before she knelt to be at Robby's level. Her mouth curved into a smile that Luke wished desperately she'd turn in his direction.

"I hadn't really thought about it," she admitted. "What would you like to call me?"

"Daddy calls you Katie."

"Except when he's mad," she confided. "Then he calls me Caitlyn."

Robby grinned. "He calls me Robert when he's mad at me. And his face gets all scrunched up. Sometimes I think he's gonna 'splode."

Katie chuckled, glancing up at Luke. "Yeah, it does look that way, doesn't it?"

"I had no idea I was so predictable," Luke commented. He looked at his son. "So, what's it going to be, sport? Do you know what you want to call Katie?"

Robby hesitated. "I guess I should call you Katie," he said with obvious reluctance.

Luke could see the disappointment on his son's face and realized that Robby really wanted to have someone in his life he could call Mommy, even if it wasn't his real mother. At the moment, though, loyalty to the absent Betty Sue kept him from admitting it.

"You know," Luke said lightly. "Whatever you decide tonight doesn't have to be your final choice. You can always change your mind."

"Absolutely," Katie agreed. "You call me whatever you feel comfortable with and anytime you want to change it's okay with me."

Robby nodded. "If you make me eat spinach, I'll probably call you Caitlyn."

Katie laughed, and for a minute the tension in the hallway seemed to ease. Peg was watching her niece with Robby, tears gathering in her eyes, and a smile on her lips. Truth be told, Luke was a little misty-eyed himself.

"Will you read me a story?" Robby asked Katie.

"It's a little late for a story," Luke protested. "Besides, I'll bet Peg already read you one."

"Two," Peg confirmed.

"But I'm going to bed all over again," Robby countered reasonably.

"Obviously he's picked up your negotiating skills," Katie said. "Come on. I'll read you a very short story."

"Something scary?" Robby asked hopefully as the two of them went up the stairs together. "I really like stuff about goblins and monsters and stuff."

"Hey, I'm not reading something that'll keep me awake all night," Katie retorted. "I was thinking more along the lines of, say, *Goldilocks and the Three Bears.*"

"That's baby stuff," Robby argued indignantly.

As Luke watched them climb the stairs side by side, a deep sense of satisfaction stole through him. It was going to work out just fine, he told himself. Katie was the perfect mother for his son. Whatever her own misgivings about their arrangement, she would do her best for Robby.

And, he thought with a renewed sense of conviction, she was the perfect wife for him, even if it was in name only at the moment.

"Luke?"

Peg brought him back to the present.

"Let's go into the living room," he suggested and led the way. When they were settled, he gazed into Peg's worried eyes. "I'm going to handle Tommy."

"How?"

"In court."

"But how will you deal with him if he shows up here? Maybe it's time you told Robby the truth, so he won't hear it by accident. It would be just like that brother of yours to blurt it out without thinking."

She was absolutely right. He'd known that. It was what had brought him racing back to Clover this afternoon. Luke groaned and buried his face in his hands. "God, what a mess! If only I'd known six years ago..."

Peg waved off the statement. "Would you have done anything differently?"

"No," he conceded. "I did what was right. I wouldn't have given up having Robby in my life for anything."

"Well, then, that's what you have to keep in mind. It'll give you the strength to do whatever it takes to keep your son with you."

"I've asked a lot of Katie."

"Then she knows," Peg said with a relieved expression. "Good."

For a moment his confidence in his plan wavered. "Am I asking too much?"

"Has she complained?"

He shook his head. "Not nearly as bitterly as I expected."

"Well, then, that should tell you something. You've thrown her a curve, but Katie's strong. More important, she loves you."

"I'm not sure I even understand that kind of love," Luke admitted candidly. "Maybe she's just resigned to her fate."

"Nonsense!" Peg reached over and patted his hand. "You'll just have to let Katie show you the way, won't you? Besides, anyone who's made the sacrifices you have for your son surely does know all there is to know about love and commitment." She stood. "I think I'd best be going. You two have plans to make. If you need anything, Luke, you give me a call. That's what family's for."

Luke regarded her ruefully. "Maybe some family," he noted dryly. "Others just seem bent on causing trouble."

When Peg had gone, Luke drew in a deep breath, then went upstairs to the room Katie had set aside for him and his son. He found Robby sound asleep, but Katie had remained curled up on the room's second twin bed, a pillow clutched in her arms, her gaze fixed on the boy opposite her. There was something so tender, so wistful in her expression that Luke's throat clogged and he felt the sting of tears in his eyes.

Suddenly he thought of all that he'd denied her—all that he'd denied both of them—by walking away six years earlier. Would he ever be able to make amends for all of that? Before he could start yet another apology, Katie glanced up and met his gaze.

"You're so lucky," she whispered, absentmindedly brushing at an errant tear. "He's a wonderful boy."

"I wish . . ." he began, but then didn't know how to finish.

Somehow, though, Katie seemed to read his mind. She reached for his hand. "So do I, but the past doesn't matter. We can't change it, anyway. We'll just have to go on from here and do the best we can."

I love you, Luke thought with a sense of wonder, though he couldn't bring himself to say the words aloud. How much would it mean to say it after all he'd done to Katie, all he'd asked of her? Besides, wasn't he the one who didn't believe in love? Perhaps what he felt was simply gratitude.

Gazing down into Katie's eyes, however, he wondered how long he could go on disbelieving in love, when he was living day in and day out with a woman who epitomized love's shining radiance and generous, accepting heart.

For all of their worrying the night before, Tommy had never shown up. Katie and Luke had stayed awake for hours listening for the doorbell and talking about inconsequential things, avoiding any of the real issues on their minds. It had been nearly dawn before they'd finally conceded that Tommy wasn't coming and had gone upstairs to their separate beds.

As Katie had lain awake in hers, she had briefly regretted the edict that had banished Luke to a room several doors away. Then she had reminded herself of precisely how he'd manipulated himself back into her life.

All things considered, Katie thought she had handled Luke's explanations about Robby rather well, in a mature, dispassionate sort of way. In the end she supposed it didn't really matter that the child wasn't Luke's. She supposed she could even admire him for taking responsibility for Tommy's irresponsible actions all those years ago, despite the way it had messed up her own dreams.

It was the fact that Luke had lied to her or, to be more precise, had left major gaps in the truth when he'd proposed, that irritated the daylights out of her. That was what kept her awake, seething with all the unspoken charges she wished she'd leveled at him when she'd first learned the whole truth. She'd been too stunned to get into it the night before. Now, though, she recognized that if she didn't get it all out of her system eventually, she'd wind up with an ulcer. Sometime after dawn she resolved to tell Luke exactly how she felt.

Now at their late breakfast, faced with the opportunity to confront him, she was suddenly less certain. Compassion welled up inside her. He looked so exhausted, so anxious about what the day would bring. He couldn't seem to tear his gaze away from his son, as if he feared what might happen if he so much as blinked.

Not until Robby was safely away from the house, on his way to the park with a very protective Mrs. Jeffers who had been briefed about Tommy, did Luke seem to let down his guard and relax. Faced with a choice between biting her tongue until the entire crisis was resolved or getting everything out into the open, Katie finally plunged in. More secrets and silences wouldn't help anyone at this stage.

"You know," she said, idly pushing her uneaten egg around on her plate. "You can't even have a decent business relationship with someone who picks and chooses which truths he's going to share."

"I never lied to you, Caitlyn," Luke said.

She suspected he had deliberately used her given name the way he always did when he wanted to make a point or, as she'd told Robby, when he was furious with her. Katie couldn't imagine what he had to be angry about. At this moment she didn't give two hoots how angry he was or why.

"No," she agreed as she stood and began clearing dishes. "You didn't lie. You just neglected to mention a few significant things. Any other little bombshells you intend to drop?"

"About my past?"

His blasé attitude had her gnashing her teeth. "About anything, dammit."

Suddenly he looked guilty as sin, a look she found extremely worrisome.

"Actually there is one thing I've been meaning to mention," he confessed. "I started to get into it last night, but you looked beat and then Robby and Peg showed up."

"What's that?" Katie asked warily. In a desperate attempt to keep busy, she searched the refrigerator until she came up with a grapefruit. Cutting out all those little sections ought to keep her hands occupied so that she wouldn't be tempted to use them to strangle Luke, whatever he had to reveal.

"I've rented out another room."

It was the last thing she'd expected him to say. She regarded him incredulously. "You've rented out a room," she repeated. "When did you have time to do this?"

"Actually, Mrs. Jeffers took care of it for me."

Katie sucked in a deep breath. No wonder they'd been engaged in such a hush-hush conversation this morning, before Mrs. Jeffers left with Robby. Katie had foolishly assumed they were talking about keeping a close eye on Luke's son. Instead, it had just been another one of Luke's conspiracies with one of her boarders.

"I suppose you paid her off, too."

"She did me a favor, that's all," Luke responded.

"How sweet of her."

Luke regarded her warily. "I thought it was. Don't you want to hear about the new tenant?"

"Oh, by all means," she snapped. "Assuming you think it's something I need to know."

"Now, Katie..."

"Oh, for heaven's sakes, get on with it, Luke."

"Okay, it's Henrietta Myers. You remember Henrietta. She leads the church choir. Mrs. Jeffers says she's getting on in years and feels she can't keep up with things at her own place." At her lack of reaction, he continued in a rush, "Anyway, she'll be moving in here at the end of the week."

Katie slammed a knife through the grapefruit in a blow that just about bounced the fruit off the counter.

She did, however, manage to keep a tight rein on her temper.

"I wasn't aware anyone had moved out. Exactly which room did you give her?" she inquired testily. Surely he hadn't tossed one of the others out to accommodate Henrietta.

"Mine," Luke said and calmly took a sip of his third cup of coffee of the morning.

"Yours," Katie repeated slowly. Of course. She should have guessed as much.

He nodded and reached for another piece of toast.

"Okay. That's good. That's very good. Another paying resident is always welcome. And I've always liked Henrietta, even though she is something of a busybody." She slanted a look at Luke, who seemed very pleased with himself. "Just one question. Where do you and Robby intend to sleep?"

"I thought I'd turn the attic into a room for Robby."

"Okay," she said. "Right now it's jammed with junk and doesn't have any insulation, but I guess that could work. And you?"

"I was planning to move into our room," he said, spreading a thick layer of strawberry preserves on his toast.

Katie smiled at him. Beamed, in fact. "When pigs fly," she said cheerfully.

"Now, Katie."

"Don't you 'now, Katie' me, Luke Cassidy. We had a deal, in writing. If I need to, I'll get it so you can read it again. It was very clear on this. You and I will not sleep together. Period." She shrugged. "Seems to me you've outsmarted yourself. Maybe you'd like to try out the hammock. You seem to be partial to it."

His blue eyes blazed. "I am not sleeping in the damned hammock."

She shrugged indifferently. "Whatever."

"Katie, I think you're carrying this crazy rule of yours to extremes. How will it look to the judge if we're in separate bedrooms?"

She glowered at him. "That is not my problem. You should have thought of it before you made the bargain. Maybe if you'd told me everything that was going on, we could have come to different terms."

"Why can't we do that now?"

"Because it's too late. A deal's a deal."

"You're just being stubborn and mule-headed," Luke accused. "What difference could it possibly make whether or not I sleep in your room? We're married, for goodness' sakes. It's hardly improper."

"Propriety was the last thing on my mind when I drew up that contract," she retorted. "You wanted a business deal. You got a business deal."

Luke suddenly reached out and snagged her hand. Before she could prevent it, he'd hauled her onto his lap.

"And now I don't," he said softly. "I want a marriage, Katie, a real one."

Katie struggled to free herself before she could succumb to that coaxing note in his voice. "Well, I don't."

"Liar," he whispered, his breath fanning across her cheek.

"That's certainly the way to win my heart," she retorted. "Calling me a liar really makes my pulse race."

He grinned unrepentantly. "Something I'm doing makes it race," he pointed out as his fingers settled at the base of her throat.

"It is racing because I am furious."

"I suppose that could be one reason," he conceded, brushing an unexpected kiss lightly across her lips. He nodded in satisfaction. "Now that really seems to kick it into gear. I wonder what a real kiss would do."

"I wouldn't try it if I were you," she warned.

"Oh?" he said, sounding amused. "What will you do? Last time, you kissed me back."

"Last time I didn't know the man kissing me was a low-down, conniving jerk."

The accusation had him grinning. "Sure, you did. You just didn't want to admit to yourself that you could fall for anyone with less than perfect personality traits."

That much was true. Under the circumstances, she didn't consider her feelings for Luke to be something to be proud of. She wouldn't admit that to him if he tried to torture it out of her. At the moment with his lips barely a hairsbreadth away and his fingers caressing the sensitive bare skin at the base of her throat, it seemed a sweet, dangerous torture was definitely on his mind. Katie was not about to submit to it willingly.

Twisting unexpectedly, she broke free and stood over him, resisting the urge to wrap her arms protectively around her middle. "This can't happen again," she said emphatically.

Luke, blast him, just laughed. "Oh, but it will, Katie. I can guarantee it."

She glowered at him. "Then you're going to have a bigger problem than Tommy's return on your hands," she snapped and fled before he could say or do anything to weaken her already wavering resolve.

Chapter Eight

"Well, if it isn't little Katie. Just look how you've grown up."

Alone in the backyard where she'd been weeding the vegetable garden, Katie shivered as the sleazily sensual tone and the voice registered. She knew without even looking that they belonged to Tommy Cassidy.

At one time she had tried valiantly to get along with Tommy because Luke had cared so deeply about his brother. But she'd never been blinded to his flaws as Luke had once been. The most offensive had been his tendency to regard all women as targets for his sly innuendoes and advances. Apparently he hadn't reformed.

Before responding to him now, she drew in a deep breath and considered exactly how she ought to deal with Luke's brother. Coolly polite seemed like the right approach under the circumstances. She certainly didn't want to do or say anything that would worsen the situation.

"Hello, Tommy," she said, turning slowly until she was face-to-face with the man responsible for Luke's distress and, indirectly anyway, for her marriage. She wasn't sure yet if that was something she ought to thank him for or not.

Feigning a nonchalance she was far from feeling, she deliberately continued watering the plants. She didn't want Tommy getting the idea that his arrival had startled her or that she viewed it as being of any consequence. Besides, if he really got out of line, she could always hose him down.

"It's been a long time," she said.

"Not long enough, isn't that what you'd like to say?" he challenged with a considering gleam in his eyes.

Those eyes were a faded shade of the same blue as Luke's. In fact, everything about Tommy seemed to be a second-best version of his older brother. Maybe he recognized that. Maybe falling short in any comparison was the real problem between him and Luke.

"Why wouldn't I be glad to see you?" Katie contradicted, forcing a smile. "You're family now."

Tommy's laughter was tinged with bitterness. "Yeah, right. I'm sure you'll invite me over to spend the holidays this year."

"You'll always be welcome here," Katie insisted, then gave him a warning look. "As long as you don't do anything to hurt your brother or our son."

For an instant he seemed taken aback by her direct-
ness. "Oh, so you've claimed Robby," he said after a
lengthy pause. "I wonder what Betty Sue would have
to say about that."

"I'm Robby's stepmother," Katie corrected. "I'd
never try to take Betty Sue's place."

"Saint Katie," he said derisively. "Maybe you and
old Luke are a match made in heaven after all."

Ignoring his sarcasm, Katie said, "I'm sure the
court will see it exactly that way." Suddenly tired of
the game, she looked Tommy straight in the eye.
"Why are you doing this? What's the point? You're
only going to hurt Robby."

"He's my boy," Tommy said in much the same
possessive way he might stake a claim to a car or, in
years past, to a bicycle or a toy.

"From what I hear you didn't care much about that
fact six years ago."

"Don't believe everything you hear."

"Are you saying you didn't run off and abandon
Betty Sue when you found out she was pregnant?"
Katie asked.

"Oh, I left," Tommy conceded. "But I thought
better of it and came back. By then, though, old Saint
Luke had taken off with my woman. He didn't leave
no forwarding address. Guess he was afraid if I
showed up, she'd leave him for a real man."

Katie didn't believe for an instant the scenario of
betrayal Tommy was painting. How dare he cast Luke
as the bad guy, she thought, when he'd been left behind to deal with another of Tommy's debacles.

"Luke Cassidy is more of a man than you'll ever be," she snapped, losing her fragile grip on her patience exactly as she had sworn to herself she wouldn't.

Tommy shook his head, his expression filled with pity. "What kind of real man would take another man's leavings?"

Stunned by the crude remark, Katie simply stared, then said softly, "I wonder how the judge will react when he hears how highly you think of this son you claim to love?"

Gesturing toward the street with the hose and not one bit concerned that she had splattered Tommy in the process, she glared at him. "I think you'd better get out of here, after all."

Tommy didn't budge. "I came to see my boy and I'm not going anywhere until I do."

"He's not here," she said, thanking God that Mrs. Jeffers hadn't brought Robby home from the park yet. "If you want to see him, you'll have to call Luke and make arrangements with him."

"And exactly where would I find my saintly brother? Inside? Surely he hasn't gone off and abandoned you in the middle of the honeymoon," he said nastily.

Exhibiting astonishing restraint, Katie refused to rise to the bait. "He has an office in the new building next door to the bank. You'll find him there."

Tommy appeared ready to offer some gloating observation on that, but before he could, Luke appeared around the side of the house. Taking in the situation at a glance, he strolled directly to Katie's side. As if it were the most natural thing in the world, he slipped an arm around her waist and dropped an affectionate kiss on her cheek. "Hey, darlin', I see we have company."

All at once Tommy didn't seem quite so sure of himself. His cocky demeanor visibly faltered for an instant, showing a fleeting glimpse of vulnerability. Suddenly thoughtful, Katie wondered if Luke recognized it. A glance at his expression told her nothing.

It hardly mattered because the change in Tommy's manner didn't last. Within seconds his jaunty, arrogant facade was back in place, leaving Katie to wonder if she'd only imagined that hint of uncertainty.

"Hey, big brother, your new bride and I were just getting reacquainted."

He managed to add a suggestive note to the comment that struck Katie as dangerous given Luke's already taxed patience with him.

"Is that right?" Luke said.

Luke studied Katie's face intently as if looking for some sign that there'd been trouble between her and his brother. She wasn't about to add to the stress of the situation by declaring that Tommy Cassidy was deliberately showing signs of behaving even more despicably than she'd thought possible.

Nor did she want to discuss the startling hint of compassion she'd felt for him minutes earlier when she'd spotted that uncertainty in his eyes. His attitude and the faint evidence of an inner turmoil struck her as being very much at odds. She wasn't certain yet which was the real Tommy. She did know that they all needed time to find out for sure.

Hoping to buy some of that time, she said mildly, "Tommy was on his way to your office to see about making arrangements to see Robby."

Katie felt Luke's entire body tense.

"Sorry, that's not possible," he said flatly, leaving no room for compromise.

Color flooded Tommy's cheeks. "Dammit, you can't keep me away from my boy."

"I can and I will, unless a judge tells me I have to do otherwise," Luke replied matter-of-factly.

Tommy's mouth twisted and his expression turned ugly. "You'll be sorry, Luke. When the shoe's on the other foot and you come begging to see Robby, I'll remember this day, and I'll see that you regret turning me away."

Katie decided enough was enough. Tempers were bound to escalate into a nasty scene if this went on much longer. Swallowing her own anger, she said, "Maybe you both should cool down. Why don't we go inside and talk this over like reasonably mature adults?"

"There's nothing to talk over," Luke declared.

"Nothing," Tommy agreed.

"Well, isn't that just peachy," Katie retorted. "Who's going to suffer because the two of you are too pig-headed to compromise? I'll tell you who. A little boy who doesn't deserve any of this. Robby's the innocent party here, and I won't have him turned into the victim of your two giant-size egos. Now get inside, sit down and talk or I swear I'll hose you both down until you cool off." She waved the garden hose in their direction to emphasize the point.

Luke stared at her for the space of a heartbeat, then unexpectedly he grinned, a gleam of admiration in his eyes. The tension in his shoulders eased a bit and he looked at his brother. "Persuasive, isn't she?"

Even Tommy seemed amused by her threat. When he smiled, the resemblance to Luke was startling.

"A regular hellcat," Tommy agreed.

"Shall we go inside?" Luke asked.

"I don't see that we have a lot of choice. I for one don't relish getting soaked to the skin."

Katie watched with satisfaction as they walked off together. She didn't hold out a lot of hope that the negotiations would be peaceful, just that they wouldn't kill each other. Maybe, given enough time, they would remember what family was supposed to be.

Luke sat across from his brother at the kitchen table and wondered for the zillionth time how Katie had managed to get the two of them inside. Surely neither he nor Tommy had actually felt threatened by that spray of water she'd been waving around. Maybe they both knew in their guts that she was right, that it was time to start talking calmly before this entire custody mess got completely out of hand. At any rate, he had to admire her audacity in forcing them to the bargaining table. If only she had come inside to keep peace, he thought as he studied Tommy warily.

Because he couldn't decide what to say, Luke got to his feet, went to the refrigerator and grabbed a pitcher of iced tea. Holding it out, he asked, "Want some?"

Tommy shook his head. "You got any beer in there?"

Luke pulled a bottle out and handed it to him without comment. He kept his opinion of drinking before noon to himself. When Tommy saw Luke watching him swig down a huge gulp, he said defensively, "It's hot as blazes out there."

"Sure is," Luke agreed readily. Determined to stay on neutral turf, he asked, "So, tell me, are you still working over in Birmingham?"

Tommy shook his head. "The job was a dead end. I thought I might go to Alaska. I hear you can make great money up there and it's gotta be cooler than this. I'm tired of being steamed like a piece of broccoli from May through October."

"Pretty damned cold up there come February, especially for a little boy," Luke said.

The comment seemed to startle Tommy, as if he'd forgotten all about the fact that he claimed he wanted his son with him. His reaction only confirmed Luke's suspicion that what Tommy really wanted was a financial stake either to get him started in Alaska or to keep him from having to work anywhere for a while.

"But I'll bet he'd love all that snow," Tommy finally countered. "You ever seen snow, big brother? Oh, wait, what am I thinking about? You probably go skiing at least twice a winter in Aspen, don't you?"

"I've never been skiing in my life," Luke retorted. "Besides, what the hell does that have to do with anything?"

Before Tommy could snap out a reply to that, Katie strolled through the door. She glanced hopefully from one to the other, but apparently she didn't like what she saw.

"Haven't you two settled anything yet?"

Luke scowled. Tommy glared.

"Terrific," she commented wearily. "Now you're not even talking." Suddenly she brightened. "Then again, maybe that's an improvement. I'll do the talking."

"Give it a rest, Katie," Luke warned quietly. "I think Tommy has made himself clear here. His terms are unacceptable."

"What terms?" Katie said.

"Money."

Tommy shot to his feet. "I never said a damned thing about wanting your money."

"But that's the bottom line, isn't it? That's what the crack about Aspen was all about, right? You want what you think I have. You just don't want to be bothered working for it they way I did."

For an instant Tommy's outraged expression gave way to something sad and lonely. Luke was taken aback by that stark look in his brother's eyes. Was there even a remote chance that he'd gotten it wrong after all?

"That is what you want, isn't it?" he repeated, hoping for a denial he could buy.

Tommy heaved a sigh. "Would you believe me if I said no?"

Luke wished he could say an unequivocal yes. He wished with all his heart that he didn't remember each and every time Tommy had sworn something to him, only to have his promises turn out to be lies. The stakes were too high this time for him to allow himself to be taken in.

"Never mind," Tommy said. "I can see the answer on your face." He turned and headed for the door. "See you in court, big brother."

The screen door slammed behind him. Only after the sound of his footsteps had faded did Luke dare a look in Katie's direction. She seemed as shaken by the outcome of the encounter as he was.

"Luke?"

"Don't even say it," he warned. "I won't start feeling sorry for him."

"But what if all he really wants is someone to love?" she asked, voicing the thought that had been taunting him for the past few minutes. "What if this isn't just about Robby, but about you, about getting your attention and your love?"

"He's always had my love," Luke said tightly. "All those years, even when everybody said I was a damned fool, Tommy had my love. He's my brother, for God's sake."

"He had it and threw it away," she pointed out. "Maybe he doesn't realize that it's still here just for the asking."

"Dammit, Katie, don't start thinking like that. Whatever his real agenda is, he's using Robby as a pawn. I doubt I'll ever be able to forgive him for that."

Before she could turn those big green eyes of hers on him and change his mind, he set his unfinished glass of tea on the table and headed for the back door. "I'm going to the park to find my son."

Though a part of him wanted to desperately, he didn't invite Katie to go with him.

"Of all the pig-headed, stubborn, mule-brained men on the face of the earth, you are at the top of the list, Luke Cassidy!"

Unfortunately there was no one in the kitchen to hear Katie's proclamation. The back door was still rattling on its hinges from Luke's exit.

Katie stood where she was, ticking off all the logical reasons Luke had to distrust his brother. But as rational as his response was, she couldn't help thinking that maybe, just this once Tommy deserved to be heard with an open mind. If he really was just using the custody suit because it was the only way he knew to get Luke's attention again, then someone had better listen before they all wound up in court. She was hardly Tommy's biggest fan, but it appeared it was up to her to get through to Luke.

She hurried upstairs, showered and changed to a pair of khaki shorts, a striped cotton blouse that she tied at the waist and sandals. Filled with determination, ten minutes later Katie was on her way to the park.

She had no trouble at all locating Luke. He was the tallest person in the small playground area with its slides and swings and colorful climbing equipment. Mrs. Jeffers had retreated to a bench in the shade under a huge old oak tree nearby. Robby was screaming with glee as Luke pushed him higher and higher in the swing.

For a moment Katie stood still and simply watched the two of them, wondering at the twist of fate that so unexpectedly had made them part of her life. She'd been married and a stepmother for little more than forty-eight hours and yet the feelings that were growing inside her were as powerful as if Luke and Robby had been a part of her life for much longer. The need to protect them from harm flooded through her as if a dam had burst in her heart.

Right now, though, the need to shake some sense into Luke was stronger. She walked over to the swings, aware that Luke's gaze was riveted to her as she approached. He didn't seem exactly thrilled to see her.

"Hi, guys," she said casually. "Having fun?"

"Wanna swing, Katie? Daddy could push you, too."

She grinned at Robby. "I think I'll pass. I might get dizzy going up as high as you. You must be part bird."

Robby nodded enthusiastically. "An eagle," he declared. "I told Daddy I wanted to soar like an eagle. We saw one once, in Colorado."

"I'll bet that was exciting."

"Mommy got scared. I don't think she liked being up on that ridge." At a look from his father, Robby's expression faltered. "Did I say something wrong?"

"Absolutely not," Katie reassured him. "I want to hear about all the things you did before I met you. Maybe we can make a deal."

The idea seemed to intrigue Robby. "What kind of deal?"

"I'll read you a story every night, after you tell me a story about something you did. That way I can share vicariously in all of the adventures you've had."

"What's vicar...vi? You know, that word you said."

Luke grinned at him. "It means that Katie hasn't had any adventures of her own, and she wants to pretend she's shared yours."

"Should I tell her about the snake?"

Katie was beginning to regret her willingness to hear about the kind of adventures that appealed to a small boy. "The snake?" she said warily.

Robby nodded sagely. "I know, you're a girl and girls don't like snakes. Mommy really, really hated that one, too."

"A sensible woman," Katie declared.

Luke shot a startled look in her direction, as if he couldn't believe that she would side with Betty Sue about anything. Their gazes caught and held, and for just a moment air between them crackled with awareness.

"Robby, why don't you go get your bike?" Luke suggested, his gaze never leaving Katie's face. "Maybe Mrs. Jeffers will go with you while you take another ride around the park."

"Yeah, she's probably all rested by now." He grinned impishly at Katie. "She says I wore her out before."

"I can imagine," Katie said.

As soon as Robby had scampered off, Luke gestured to the swing he'd vacated. "Have a seat. I promise you won't get dizzy."

Too late, Katie thought. Her head was spinning from the provocative gleam she'd seen in Luke's eyes. Still, she took the seat he'd offered and allowed him to give her a slow, steady push until she was soaring almost as high as Robby. On the descent, Luke captured the swing and held it so that her back was pressed against his chest.

"Giddy yet?" he inquired softly, his breath fanning across her cheek.

Katie's pulse bucked at the seductive teasing. "Steady as a rock," she claimed.

"Then what are those goose bumps doing on your arms?" he taunted.

"It's chilly."

Luke's laughter rippled over her. "It's ninety-five degrees out here, and the humidity must be close to that."

"It was ninety-eight yesterday," she countered. "There's been a break in the weather."

"Not enough to account for those goose bumps. Must be something else."

She took a huge risk with her already wavering equilibrium and leaned back against his chest. "Such as?"

He slowly trailed a finger up her arm. "Maybe that?"

Katie shivered.

"Gotcha!" Luke murmured triumphantly.

She twisted in the swing until she could gaze up into his face. "There was never any question that you could get a response out of me," she admitted. "That was true six years ago and it's true now. The big difference is that now I'm old enough and wise enough not to act on that response."

Before he could challenge her on that, she slid out of the swing and stood facing him. "I came here to talk, not to play games."

Luke's expression sobered at once. "Forget it. I don't want to discuss Tommy."

"Then don't. Just listen. Are you willing to risk the opportunity to settle this before Robby ever finds out just because you're too stubborn to keep an open mind about your brother's motives?"

Luke scowled at her. "Weren't you the one who used to tell me repeatedly that I was too lenient, that I gave Tommy the benefit of the doubt too often?"

"That was then. This is now."

"What's the difference? Tommy hasn't changed."

"Maybe he has, maybe he hasn't. You won't know for sure until you've spent some time with him."

"I can't risk letting him around Robby."

"Then spend time with him away from the house. Take him fishing. Give him a job. Whatever it takes for you to get to know him again. Judge for yourself what his real motive is."

"I know..."

Katie shook her head. "You're reacting with all the pain and anger you felt when he ran off six years ago and left you to deal with Betty Sue."

"It's not just what happened back then. He's threatening to take my son."

"But you may be able to stop him."

"Exactly. In court."

Katie shook her head. "Maybe just by giving him his family back."

"I can't take that risk," Luke said with an edge of desperation in his voice as his gaze sought out his son who was pedaling his bike like crazy while Mrs. Jeffers struggled to keep up with him.

"You can't not take it," Katie countered.

"I married you to keep Tommy out of our lives. Now you want me to welcome him back," he said, running his fingers through his hair in a gesture of frustration. "What the hell went wrong?"

Katie ignored the pain that sliced through her at his blunt assessment of his reason for marrying her. Forcing a grin, she shrugged. "Hey, if you misjudged me, maybe you've misjudged Tommy, too."

She watched as he struggled to accept her challenge. A part of her wished he would ignore her pleas. Because if it turned out she was wrong about his brother, she knew without a doubt that she would lose Luke for the second time in her life. This time she wasn't sure she would ever recover.

Chapter Nine

The next morning Katie figured that as long as she was back in Clover anyway and wide awake, she might as well go in for her regular shift at Peg's Diner. Despite Luke's promised bailout of the boarding house, she wanted to contribute as much as possible to the upkeep. She was determined that Luke not mistake for one minute that it was her business.

Peg was still checking the setups of napkins, salt, pepper and sugar on all the tables when Katie unlocked the diner's front door just past dawn. The aroma of freshly brewed coffee scented the air. Katie headed straight for the pot and poured herself a cup before Peg could even manage to snap her mouth shut.

"And just what do you think you're doing in here?" Peg inquired, facing her down, eyes blazing.

"Unless you've fired me, I work here."

"You're on your honeymoon."

Katie shrugged. "We're home. I figured I might as well get back into my regular routine."

Just then the sound of another key being turned in the front door had Katie spinning around. She turned just in time to see Ginger catch sight of her and freeze, her expression uncertain. Katie stared at her teenaged boarder.

"What are you doing here?"

Ginger regarded Katie with dismay, then turned to Peg. "You didn't tell her?"

"Tell me what?" Katie demanded.

Peg sighed heavily. "Well, the truth of it is that I hired Ginger to take your place."

"You mean while I was out of town," Katie said slowly, looking from one to the other. Both women looked guilty as sin. She began to get the idea that she was not going to like any further elaboration they offered.

"Not exactly," Peg admitted. "Actually, I figured now that you're married and have Robby and all, you'd be too busy to be carrying a full load here the way you were doing before."

"So you fired me?" Katie said incredulously. "Without even talking to me about it?"

"I didn't fire you," Peg insisted.

"Just replaced me."

"I cut back on your hours," she countered.

"How far back?" Katie challenged. "You know this place can't afford to keep two waitresses on the payroll besides you." She glanced at Ginger's crestfallen expression. "Ginger, would you mind leaving me alone with my aunt for a minute?"

"Sure, Katie. I'll help Sonny in the kitchen." She rushed through the swinging door to the back as if she couldn't get away from the tension-filled atmosphere fast enough.

"You're not telling me everything, are you?" Katie demanded. "You wouldn't do something like this all on your own. I'm practically your own flesh and blood, for goodness' sakes. You wouldn't just toss me out on my rear end without someone putting you up to it."

"I don't know what you mean," Peg replied, looking everywhere but into Katie's eyes. Her hand was shaking so badly, she'd spilled more salt all over the table, than she'd gotten into the shaker.

Katie recognized all the signs indicating the depth of her aunt's distress. Normally Peg was as steady-handed and direct as any person on the face of the earth. "Peg, you are my aunt and I love you, but you are a pitiful liar. This was Luke's idea, wasn't it?"

Finally Peg's gaze clashed directly with hers. "Well, for once, I agreed with him," she said with a touch of defiance. "You were working yourself to death before. It'll only be worse now, if you try to keep doing everything."

Indignation and outrage boiled over inside Katie. "If I want to work myself to death, it's my decision," she practically shouted. Forcing herself to lower her voice, she said, "Dammit, I like being busy. I like working with you. I like talking to the customers."

Peg's determined expression faltered. "I had no idea it would even matter to you," she said. "If I had...well, I have no idea what I would have done. Luke was very persuasive."

"Did he offer to pay Ginger's salary?" Katie inquired irritably.

Peg looked shocked by the question. "Why on earth would he do a thing like that?"

"Force of habit," Katie said. "He seems to think he can buy whatever he wants in life."

"Meaning?" Peg asked, studying her with a speculative expression.

Katie sighed heavily. That was one question she had no intention of answering. A totally honest reply would only upset her aunt. "Nothing. Don't mind me. I just resent what he did."

"He couldn't have done it without my cooperation," Peg pointed out. "I sincerely regret that I gave it to him. I really am sorry, sweetheart. I'll speak with Ginger."

Suddenly the last of the fight drained out of Katie. "You can't fire her. She needs the money."

"But you're right," Peg argued. "I shouldn't have made a decision like this without talking it over with you. Luke and I just thought it was for the best." She brightened slightly. "Maybe both of you could stay on, take fewer hours. It's summer, anyway. We're always busier this time of year. Then in the fall, when Ginger's back in school, we'll reevaluate."

Katie realized then that it was awfully silent in the kitchen. Usually by this time in the morning Sonny was slamming pots and pans around and singing at the top of his lungs. She had a hunch, though, that today he and Ginger were both hanging on every word she and Peg were speaking.

"I suppose we could try it," she agreed, loudly enough to be overheard by anyone who just happened to be listening. "As long as we're not bumping into each other in the aisles, it should be okay."

Without waiting to be beckoned, Ginger rushed through the swinging door, a relieved smile spreading across her face. She threw her arms around Katie. "Thank you. I never meant to upset you. I guess I figured I'd be helping Peg out of a jam and earning some college money at the same time."

Katie hugged her back. "None of this was your doing. It just seems my family has a tendency to make decisions for me." She glanced pointedly at Peg. "At least my aunt knows now that this is a very bad idea."

Peg grinned at her and nodded. "You've made yourself perfectly clear to me. I'm not so sure I want to be around, though, when Luke finds out."

Her concern was well-founded. Apparently the minute Luke figured out that Katie was nowhere in the boarding house, he yanked Robby out of bed and came storming over to the diner. His clothes rumpled, his hair uncombed, Robby appeared slightly dazed by the rude awakening. Katie winked at him as he passed by, but ignored her husband.

Luke took one look at Katie serving a table of tourists and turned a furious gaze on Peg.

Peg apparently wasn't one bit daunted by his scowling demeanor. She shrugged. "Take it up with your wife."

"Oh, I intend to," he said, heading straight for a booth. He nudged Robby in ahead of him, then kept his gaze fastened on Katie with a blazing look that could have set half the town afire if the sparks had gone astray.

Katie decided this was not a discussion she cared to have in the middle of the diner with the entire town of Clover certain to hear the details before lunchtime. The decibel level was likely to reach a peak that could shatter glass. Still seething with resentment, she sent Ginger over to wait on him.

Ginger was back behind the counter in a heartbeat. "He wants you," she said in a hushed tone.

"Well, he can't have me. That's not my station."

"Actually it is," Ginger pointed out.

Katie frowned at her. "Our agreement can be canceled just like that," she said with a snap of her fingers. At Ginger's terrified expression she relented. "Oh, never mind. I'll go. Give me the coffeepot."

"I've already poured the coffee," Ginger said in a way that suggested Katie might not be trusted to pour it into a cup.

Katie plucked her order pad out of her pocket and marched over to Luke's booth. She saved her friendly grin for Robby.

"Just get up?" she asked him.

"Daddy was in a hurry. He didn't even make me brush my teeth," he said with obvious amazement over his good luck.

"I wonder why," Katie said sweetly, still not glancing at her husband. "So, what are you having?"

"A conversation with my wife," Luke said in a low, lethal tone.

"Sorry, not on the menu. The special this morning is a Western omelette."

"Fine, whatever," Luke snapped.

"I want pancakes," Robby said, oblivious to the undercurrents. "It's really neat coming here for breakfast. I can have pancakes anytime I want. Daddy burns them."

"I do not burn them," Luke said testily.

"You should see what he does to eggs," Robby added, not the least bit intimidated by his father's foul mood.

"Well, fortunately, Sonny is a whiz with pancakes and eggs," Katie said. "I like coming here for breakfast, too."

"I can't imagine when you find the time to eat it," Luke said.

"Do I look as if I'm starving?" Katie retorted.

The question was a mistake. She knew it the moment the words were out of her mouth. Luke slowly, deliberately surveyed her from head to toe with a provocative consideration that had her skin practically sizzling. Dear heaven! She barely resisted the urge to fan herself with a menu. "Nope, you do have a few curves," he observed generously. "More than I recalled, in fact."

"Thanks so much."

"Good color in your cheeks, too," he commented, grinning.

"Oh, go to—" She stopped herself in the nick of time, plastered a phony smile on her face and stalked off to place the order.

Unfortunately Sonny was one of the best short order cooks in the business. He had Luke and Robby's food ready before Katie could gather the composure necessary to fool all of the interested observers into thinking that she and Luke were not having their first marital tiff.

"I hope you're enjoying yourself," Luke said, when she thumped the plates onto the table.

She eyed him warily. "Are you trying to make a point?"

"It's your last day," he said, taking his first bite of omelette. "This is terrific, by the way."

"I'll give Sonny your compliments." Then added cheerfully, "And I wouldn't bet on this being my last day, if I were you. You'd lose."

"We'll see."

He said it so smugly, as if there were some angle she hadn't considered, that it gave Katie pause. Regarding him speculatively, she moved on to another table. If he wanted more coffee or more anything, too bad, she thought with a touch of defiance. She'd spend her energy on customers who appreciated her waitressing skills. Luke probably wouldn't even leave a tip. He probably thought he'd already tipped her well enough by depositing that check into her account.

The next time she glanced toward Luke's booth, it was well after nine o'clock. He was sitting there scribbling notes on a tablet he'd apparently filched from

Peg's supply under the cash register. There was no sign of Robby.

With only one other customer in the place chatting happily with Ginger at the counter, Katie couldn't think of a single way to go on avoiding her husband. She poured herself a cup of coffee and carried it with her to his table, then slid in opposite him. He glanced up.

"All done making your point?" he inquired.

"And what point would that be?"

"That I can't run your life."

Katie regarded him intently. "I'm not sure. Have I gotten it through that thick skull of yours yet?"

"Only the first layer. Maybe you'd better try explaining to me why you want to work yourself to death this way."

Okay, Katie thought, that was a reasonable enough request. She tried to formulate an explanation that wouldn't cause him to order her to shut down the boarding house instead. Luke seemed to have turned into an either-or sort of guy. She had to make him see that both jobs were essential to her.

"I love the boarding house," she began. "I poured all of my energy into it."

"To say nothing of your money," he reminded her.

She frowned at him and he held up his hands. "Sorry," he said. "Go on."

"But Ginger and the others all have their own lives. Sometimes I just need a break from all the quiet, from doing laundry and dusting. I like coming in here and hearing what's going on around town. I like meeting the tourists. Plus I owe Peg. I get a sense of satisfaction from being able to pay her back in some small way for all she did for me. Having the boarding house and the diner gives me a sort of balance in my life.''

To Luke's credit he listened to every word she said, but his expression grew bleaker by the minute. Katie didn't understand his reaction.

''You still don't understand, do you?'' she asked.

''I understand,'' he said flatly. Blue eyes met hers. ''But where in this equation do Robby and I fit in?''

Katie felt as if all the breath had whooshed right out of her. ''Is that what you're worried about? That I won't have time for the two of you?''

''There are only twenty-four hours in a day,'' he reminded her. ''You're already cramming them to the max.''

Katie was stunned that he would think that he and his son would get only whatever leftover minutes she could salvage from an already overburdened schedule. Maybe what astonished her even more was the fact that it really seemed to matter to him at all.

''I suppose I hadn't thought about how it would seem to you,'' she admitted honestly. She looked directly into his eyes. ''But, Luke, you and Robby will always be my first priority. I meant every word I said when we took our vows.''

He was regarding her doubtfully. ''Every word?''

''Of course.''

''What about obey?'' he teased, his expression suddenly lighter.

''That word was never spoken,'' she retorted.

''Oh, I'm certain it was. Love, honor and obey, wasn't that it? I'm sure Justice of the Peace Abernathy read from a very traditional version of the ceremony."

"Absolutely not. I would have remembered."

He grinned and reached for her hand, lacing his fingers through hers. "You do remember the love and honor part, though?"

"Vaguely," she murmured, barely able to concentrate for all the dangerous sensations rioting through her.

"Maybe we should talk about that in more detail later, when we're alone," Luke suggested.

"Uh-huh," Katie managed when she could catch her breath. This was not good, not good at all. "I'd better go now."

Luke's grin widened. "Where?"

She shook her head to clear it, then glanced desperately around for someplace, anyplace she might be needed in a very big hurry. "The kitchen," she said hurriedly. "I have to help clean up in the kitchen."

"All done," Peg sang out.

"Now what?" Luke inquired with that lazy, smug expression firmly back in place.

"I have to go..." she racked her brain "...to the store. I have to get food for the boarders."

"They're staying at the hotel, remember?"

"That's ridiculous," Katie countered. "I'll tell them to come home. They shouldn't be spending their money on hotel rooms, when they've already paid me."

"I'm paying for their rooms," Luke said. "I'm sure Mr. O'Reilly's in heaven with room service at his command. You wouldn't want to spoil it for him, would you?''

She sighed. ''I suppose not.''

Luke gave a little nod of satisfaction, then stood, leaned down and kissed her in a slow, leisurely fashion that melted every single bone in her body. ''I'll be waiting for you at home.''

Thoroughly dazed, Katie simply stared after him as he strolled from the diner.

''Whew!'' Ginger said, emerging from the kitchen waving a dish towel in front of her face. ''That man is hot enough to fry bacon.'' Realizing what she'd said and about whom, she winced and turned an apologetic look on Katie. ''Sorry.''

''For what?'' Peg interjected. ''Appreciating a man who could turn the Arctic into steam heat?'' At Katie's look of astonishment, she added, ''Well, it's true. Luke does have a certain way about him.''

A possessive smile crept over Katie's face. ''Yes,'' she said finally. ''He does indeed have a way about him.''

She just wished she could be sure there was more to it than inbred flirtatiousness or the desperation of a man who needed to present an impression of marital bliss to a judge.

Luke sat in his new office, surrounded by all the most modern equipment, and tried to make sense of what had just happened with Katie. He'd been toying with the same question for more than an hour now. He'd bought controlling stock in entire corporations with less consideration.

The truth of it was his new wife was a puzzle to him. He couldn't begin to imagine how that had come about. After all, Katie was his oldest and dearest friend. He'd been her first lover, though he realized he had no idea if he'd been her last. At any rate, nothing about her should be taking him by surprise. That was the main reason he'd come home determined to marry her. He was sick to death of surprises.

To his astonishment, though, she wasn't the same adoring, compliant woman he'd left behind. She had a mind of her own. She'd learned to take care of herself. In fact, except for cleaning up the financial mess she'd gotten herself into with the boarding house, she didn't seem to need him at all.

Which made him wonder why she'd accepted his proposal. She could have fixed things at the bank. Despite his tough talk, bank president Charlie Hastings would walk over burning coals for Katie. Katie had probably known it, too.

Instead, she had agreed to marry Luke, become stepmother to his son and negotiated what had to be the oddest prenuptial agreement on record. Or not on record to be more precise, since they were the only people who knew about it, unless Katie had gotten it into her head to file the document at City Hall. He realized he wasn't so sure this new Katie wouldn't do exactly that.

Katie was turning out to be far less predictable than he'd anticipated. She was absolutely bursting with surprises. It was a rude discovery for a man who'd been praying for a little stability in his life. He'd come home looking for a tame old friend and found himself married to a hellion.

Yet Luke had to admit he was intrigued with this new Katie. He'd been physically attracted to the old Katie, and that much hadn't changed. But this new, fascinating woman stimulated him in ways he hadn't expected. In fact, just thinking about the way Katie had stood in the middle of Peg's Diner and blatantly defied him turned him on.

Maybe even more important, it made him smile. Ever since Tommy had declared his intent to gain custody of Robby, Luke hadn't had all that much to smile about. Now he had Katie, who made his blood race just by going toe-to-toe with him and standing up for herself. Given his penchant for taking charge and her determination to control her own destiny, he figured more battles were a certainty. In fact, he looked forward to them.

Suddenly smiling to himself, he tossed down his pen and headed for the door. It shouldn't take him more than an hour or so back at the boarding house to find something to change. With any luck he ought to be able to stir up another one of those stimulating clashes before dinnertime.

Chapter Ten

It didn't take long for Luke to find exactly what he was looking for at the boarding house. He found that the way to take charge and at the same time drive Katie nuts was in plain view under the June receipts. It was already the tenth of the month and Ginger had yet to pay her rent. Mrs. Jeffers and Mr. O'Reilly paid by the week and both were behind, though only by a few days. The pattern set off alarm bells in his head.

He went back and found that Ginger hadn't paid rent on a single occasion he could find. The other two paid, but always after some delay. It seemed the only record he could find of people actually paying what they owed, when they owed it, was of the handful of people who were passing through Clover.

Luke resolved to have a chat with all three of the regulars about the need to get the boarding house cash flow back on a sound financial base. No doubt Katie would be incensed by his interference. He could hardly wait for another one of their highly charged encounters.

In fact, he decided, why put it off? All three were likely to be at the Clover Street Hotel—at his expense. Maybe it would be better to have this conversation on neutral turf and away from Katie's interference. She was at the root of the problem. Everyone knew she was a soft touch. No doubt they played on her sympathy with endless excuses.

He experienced a momentary pang of guilt for leaving Katie out of the meeting, but he ignored it. He had no doubts at all that she would hear about it soon enough. And there was no mistaking his perverse desire to be the target of more of those sparks she threw off when she was angry.

He had no difficulty at all in tracking down two of his quarry. Mrs. Jeffers was playing a cutthroat game of checkers with Robby at a table in the lobby. John O'Reilly was in the dining room with a hamburger and fries in front of him.

Luke asked each of them if they'd seen Ginger. Mr. O'Reilly claimed he hadn't seen her since the reception at the boarding house.

"I thought she was working at the diner," Mrs. Jeffers offered.

"I saw her go upstairs," Robby said. "I think she has a class this afternoon or something. She probably had to study." He turned a puzzled look on his father. "Why does she have to go to school during the summer? I thought everybody had vacation now."

"Because she really wants to get into a good college and she's taking these summer prep classes. She wants to take at least one class each summer, hoping that she'll qualify for a scholarship," Mrs. Jeffers explained. "That's the only way she'll ever be able to afford to get a degree."

Thinking about Ginger struggling to get into college against the odds made Luke stop for a minute to consider what he was about to do. Then he thought of Katie, struggling equally hard to stay afloat, and his resolve strengthened.

"I'll give Ginger a call on the hotel's house phone," he said. "I'd like to have a minute with all of you. Mr. O'Reilly will join us as soon as he's finished his lunch."

Mrs. Jeffers instantly looked worried. "Is everything okay? You haven't changed your mind about us staying on at the boarding house, have you? I'm sure you and Katie would like to have your privacy, but we all love it there."

Robby shot a look of alarm at his father. "They have to stay, Daddy."

This wasn't going nearly as smoothly as he'd intended. Withstanding Robby's accusing looks was far worse than dealing with Katie's disapproval. "Of course, everyone is staying," he reassured them. "It's just that there's something I thought we should talk about."

"Will Katie be here?" Mrs. Jeffers asked.

"No."

"But shouldn't she be in on this?" Mrs. Jeffers protested. "It is her boarding house, after all."

Luke thought how reassured Katie would be to hear one of her boarders talking this way. "I'm just trying to save her some worry," he promised. "I'll fill her in later."

"If you say so, dear," Mrs. Jeffers said, though she still sounded doubtful.

It was nearly two o'clock by the time Luke had everyone where he wanted them, in a secluded alcove in the hotel lobby where they could have some privacy.

"I was just going over the boarding house books this morning," he began. Immediately the expressions on the faces of all three boarders fell. Obviously they guessed where this was heading. "I'm sure it's just slipped your minds, but it seems that everyone is behind in paying the rent."

"But Katie knew..." Ginger began.

"Katie always..." Mrs. Jeffers chimed in.

"Now see here, young man. I don't know that this is any business of yours," John O'Reilly stated flatly. "We've all made our arrangements with Katie."

This was not going at all the way Luke had hoped. He'd been certain that once they saw how their lackadaisical attitudes toward financial matters hurt Katie, they'd all want to help her out.

"Maybe I'm not making myself clear," he said.

"Oh, I think you are," Mr. O'Reilly countered. "Pay up or get out, isn't that it?"

"No, of course not," Luke protested.

"Sounds that way to me," the retired fireman said.

"Me, too, dear," Mrs. Jeffers concurred.

Only Ginger was silent, possibly because huge tears were spilling down her pale cheeks. Luke suddenly felt like a heel. It seemed his good intentions were backfiring. He rushed on to try to set things straight before he really botched things up.

"I'm not trying to bully you," he said. "I'm just worried about Katie."

As if a switch had been flipped, they were suddenly attentive.

"What's the matter with Katie?" Ginger asked. "She's not sick, is she?"

"Well, no, but..."

"Is she upset?" Mrs. Jeffers asked.

"Not with you all," Luke replied candidly.

"Well, for heaven's sakes, spit it out, boy," Mr. O'Reilly ordered. "You know we care about Katie. She's family."

"She could lose the boarding house," he said bluntly.

His announcement was greeted with shock. The gasp he heard, however, could not be attributed to any of the three people in front of him. In fact, he had a very strong suspicion that it came from the very woman under discussion.

Apparently his guess was far more accurate than his understanding of boarding house politics, because all three people jumped to their feet and rushed to encompass Katie in hugs, while murmuring appropriate expressions of sympathy and worry. He seemed to have been forgotten—or simply dismissed as the bearer of bad tidings.

When he finally got a glimpse of Katie's face through the cluster of clucking sympathizers, his gaze clashed with green eyes that blazed with outrage. Glancing away from that look of condemnation, he suddenly realized that his son was mysteriously absent from the scene. He guessed that the little traitor had found some way to get word of the meeting to Katie.

"I'm so sorry I wasn't here when the meeting started," Katie said, urging everyone back to their places. "I was a little late in hearing about it."

"Actually, Luke said—" Mrs. Jeffers began.

Luke jumped in. "I thought I could handle it."

"If you'd handled it much better, everyone would have moved out by nightfall, according to my source," Katie replied sweetly.

Luke vowed to gag his son in the future. Maybe he ought to blindfold him and make him wear earplugs while he was at it.

"So, what's the topic?" Katie inquired. "The impending foreclosure on my bank loan?"

She said it with an edge of sarcasm that sent a dull red flush creeping up Luke's neck. He could feel his skin burning.

"So it's true," Mr. O'Reilly said, his expression grim.

"It might have been a few weeks ago," Katie conceded. She beamed at them, but saved her most saccharine smile for Luke. "But I had a windfall that saved the day and I'm fairly certain that it was just the beginning. Everything's under control."

"For the moment," Luke said ominously.

Katie glared at him. "The situation is under control," she repeated. "You all are not to worry. You know how these uptight financial types are." She directed a pointed look at Luke. "They panic at the slightest little blip in the cash-flow pattern."

"Somebody has to," Luke muttered.

"Perhaps you and I should discuss this in private," Katie suggested.

"Perhaps we should," Luke agreed, his blood already racing at the prospect of another heated exchange with his wife. If this was the only sort of passion she intended to permit the two of them, then he intended to take full advantage of it. The evening that stretched out before them seemed open to all sorts of fascinating possibilities.

Katie couldn't understand why Luke appeared so pleased by the prospect of fighting with her. He had to know that she wasn't going to let this little incident pass without comment. Calling a meeting without telling her about it had been a sneaky, underhanded thing to do. Thank heavens for Robby! Even though he hadn't understood exactly what the discussion was all about, he'd reacted to everyone else's panic. He'd had no trouble convincing the hotel desk clerk to call Katie for him.

The walk back to the boarding house was made in silence. Katie could hardly wait to get her indignation at Luke's latest high-handiness off her chest, but Main Street was no place to do it. On that much at least, Luke apparently agreed. He hadn't even wanted

Robby as a witness. He'd sent his son off to Peg's for
the night.

Obviously, though, he was spoiling for a fight. He
had to have known that calling that meeting would
infuriate her and yet he'd deliberately gone ahead with
it. Clearly, he hadn't learned a blasted thing from their
conversation in the diner that morning. He intended
to control her life, take over her boarding house and
leave her with nothing to do.

As they neared the house, Katie's steps began to
falter. Her temper cooled a fraction. She compared
what Luke had done to what she had plotted behind
his back that very afternoon. He didn't know it yet,
but they were probably just about even. He might even
have a slight edge when it came to justifiable outrage.

The timing was lousy for her to make her announcement, but a glance at her watch told her there
was no way around it. She figured she'd better make
it while they were still on the sidewalk in front of the
boarding house, in plain view of the neighbors. This
was one time when witnesses might save her hide.

"Luke?"

He scowled at her. "I don't want to get into this out
here. We'll discuss it inside."

"In a minute. First, there's something you need to
know."

"Fine. Tell me inside."

She stopped right where she was. "I'd rather tell you
out here."

He met her gaze, his expression suddenly wary.
"Why? What's this about?"

"I just thought you ought to know..." She swallowed hard as she met his glittering blue eyes. "I've done something."

"What?"

She plastered a bright smile on her face. "I've invited Tommy for a barbecue," she blurted out.

Luke couldn't have looked more stunned if she'd announced that she was pregnant with triplets.

"You what?" he asked slowly, as if her words hadn't been perfectly clear.

"Your brother's coming over." She glanced nervously at her watch. "In about an hour."

"Oh, no, he's not," Luke countered. "Call him and cancel."

"I can't. I don't know where he is."

"You found him to issue the invitation. You can find him to cancel it."

She shook her head. "Actually, he came into the diner for lunch."

He stared at her with an expression of complete bafflement written all over his face. "Why would you do this? How dare you meddle in something that is none of your business?"

Katie couldn't believe her ears. "Excuse me? You self-righteous son of a hound dog. Who was it who just called a meeting of my tenants without telling me? If you want to talk about meddling, let's talk about that!"

"Not out here," Luke said tightly.

"Why the hell not?"

"Because half the neighborhood is hanging on every word."

"So what? Witnesses might not be such a bad idea."

"That's enough, Katie."

Luke's voice carried a low warning that she ignored. "Enough? It's not enough by a long shot. I have plenty to say about that stunt you just pulled at the hotel."

Before she could even formulate the first thought, though, Luke tucked one arm under her knees, another under her bottom and scooped her into the air. She landed against his chest with a *whoosh*.

"You low-down, rotten..." she began, kicking futilely in an attempt to cause him to lose his balance as he strode up the walk toward the house.

She heard a distinct, low, rumbling sound coming from Luke's chest that silenced her. She gazed into his eyes and saw sparks of pure mischief suddenly dancing in the blue depths.

"You're laughing," she accused.

He swallowed hard and tried for a sober expression. Unfortunately he couldn't seem to keep his lips from quirking into a smile.

"How dare you!" she said indignantly. "This is not a laughing matter."

Inside the boarding house he headed straight for the living room, seemingly oblivious to her protests. He settled onto the chintz-covered sofa, keeping Katie pinned firmly in place in his lap. Having his arms around her was beginning to have a neutralizing effect on her anger. It was hard to stay furious when every single part of her anatomy was tingling with awareness of the man who held her. It was absurd, really, how easily Luke was able to distract her.

Of course, she decided thoughtfully, he didn't seem as upset, either. In fact, he seemed to have forgotten all about his brother's impending arrival. He seemed much more interested in her bare midriff, where her blouse had ridden up. He was tracing a lazy pattern across the skin that had her insides trembling.

"Um, Luke," she said breathlessly. "This is a bad idea."

He ignored her and began tracing the neckline of her blouse which she'd left open about one button too far. Maybe two buttons too far. She probably should have sewn the damned thing together, given the way her pulse was kicking up.

"Luke, please," she said, trying to swat his hand away.

Without a word, he captured her hand and planted a deliberately provocative kiss against the sensitive palm. Katie's resistance melted. Another thirty seconds of this sweet torment and her blood would be sizzling. She wriggled in a half-hearted attempt to get free, but immediately realized that wriggling was a very bad idea. It had a prompt and unmistakable effect on Luke, that did not bode well for lowering the out-of-control heat rising between them with anything short of an icy shower.

"Luke," she murmured in her least effective attempt yet to get his attention.

"Ah, Katie," he said with a sigh as he kissed a spot on her neck just below her ear.

Katie shivered, which he must have taken as an invitation. He scattered kisses from the base of her throat to her chin, from her forehead to her cheeks, from the tip of her nose to her lips. Her mouth opened, formed his name, but not a sound emerged before she was caught up in the slow, sensual feel of Luke's velvet lips against her own. Her arms crept around his neck, her fingers tangled in his thick hair as she gave herself over to the kiss.

The touch of his mouth against hers, the beckoning heat that stole through her, set off a riot of memories. Sweet, wicked, dangerous memories. For what seemed an eternity, Katie indulged herself in sensation, accepting, provoking, hungering for more. She was swept away on the tide of tenderness. She lost herself to need, Luke's and her own.

A gentle, insistent caress of her breast sent her pulse scrambling. The slow slide of Luke's hand from calf to inner thigh made her heart thunder in her chest. Her entire body throbbed with a desperate yearning to know again this man who'd branded her heart as his own years ago.

She could fight it. She could pretend that she didn't want what was happening between them, but the truth of it was that she did. She wanted Luke to make love to her, wanted him to possess her as he once had. She hungered for it illogically, in a way that ignored past hurts and present problems, in a way that didn't give a damn for the emotional consequences. Every fiber of her being was straining toward fulfillment of a dream she'd thought only weeks ago would elude her forever. Logic and reason had nothing to do with it. All that mattered was a love that had never died.

Katie gave up the battle, gave herself over to the joy of the moment . . . just in time to hear footsteps on the front porch, a loud knock on the screen door.

"What the hell?" Luke muttered, clearly dazed and definitely unhappy about the untimely interruption.

"Tommy," she guessed, untangling herself from Luke and rising unsteadily to her feet. She straightened her clothes as she went to the door. There was nothing she could do about the flood of color in her cheeks.

Naturally Tommy couldn't let her obvious state of arousal pass without comment. His blue eyes filled with insolent amusement. "I could come back later, if I'm interrupting anything," he offered.

"Or not at all," Luke said, coming up behind Katie.

Katie saw the flash of hurt in Tommy's eyes, before he covered it with belligerence. "Or not at all," he agreed. "It's up to Katie. It's her house. I don't go where I'm not wanted."

Fully aware of Luke's disapproving scowl, she determinedly pushed open the screen door. "Of course you're wanted. I invited you, didn't I? We were late getting here. We're just running a little behind."

Tommy seemed eager to accept the explanation. Never once glancing at his brother, he asked Katie, "What can I do to help? If the grill's out back, I can start the coal."

"Terrific. I'm lousy at it," she said, leading the way to the kitchen. "Luke, why don't you help him?"

Luke looked as if he'd rather eat dirt. Shooting her a wry look, he dutifully followed his brother out the door.

The instant he'd gone, Katie's knees seemed to give way. She sank onto a chair and released the breath she'd been holding. Sweet, heavenly days, what had she been thinking in the other room?

Of course, the point was that she hadn't been *thinking* at all. She'd been giving her hormones free rein. It appeared she owed Tommy Cassidy a debt of gratitude. His arrival had just saved her from what could have been the second most costly mistake of her life.

She listened to the low, halting murmur of voices from the backyard and gave a little nod of satisfaction. Maybe she was already repaying him by giving him time to win back Luke's love and approval.

Chapter Eleven

Luke couldn't decide whether to be more furious with his brother for showing up just when he had Katie on the brink of making love with him or with his wife for inviting Tommy in the first place. It was a toss-up.

But the bottom line was that Tommy was here and there didn't seem much likelihood that anything short of a shotgun would persuade him to leave. Katie, with her strong notions about family loyalty, would definitely frown on his waving a gun threateningly at his brother.

At the moment, Tommy was working intently on getting the grill started. For the first time Luke took a minute to study him with at least some semblance of objectivity. He realized with a sense of shock that

Tommy was far too thin, practically gaunt, in fact. His skin was a pasty color that didn't look healthy.

"Are you okay?" he asked, drawing a surprised look.

"I'm fine."

"You look like hell. When was the last time you had a decent meal?"

"Today at lunch," Tommy said too quickly.

At the diner, Luke realized and wondered if Katie had paid for whatever Tommy had eaten. More than likely. "Before that," he said.

Tommy shrugged. "Sometime yesterday, I guess."

"Have you been drinking away your money?" Luke asked, thinking of the beer Tommy had asked for the morning before.

The question drew more emotion than Luke had anticipated. Tommy whirled away from the grill and glared at him.

"You know damn well I don't drink, not after the way Dad was," Tommy said heatedly. "An occasional beer is about it. That one I had yesterday was the first in weeks."

Something about his indignant tone rang true. It was hardly surprising that Tommy rarely touched alcohol. Neither did Luke. Watching their father's bouts with the stuff, seeing his dissolution before he'd finally taken off and abandoned them all would make anyone with sense wary.

Luke still wasn't sure what the explanation was for Tommy's appearance, but it instinctively worried him. Apparently old habits died harder than he thought. "You're sure you're not sick?"

"I am not sick," Tommy repeated emphatically, then shot him a wry look. "Though it would probably serve your purposes better if I were."

"What the hell is that supposed to mean?"

"Just that you could use it in court as further evidence of my unsuitability to be a parent to my boy."

"How can you even say such a thing? I wasn't looking for ammunition," Luke protested. "You look lousy. I wanted to know why." Suddenly an explanation came to him, one that would answer a lot of the questions he had about Tommy's motivations of late. "You said you left your job in Birmingham?"

Tommy regarded him resentfully. "Yeah, so what? I told you I'm heading to Alaska just as soon as this stuff with Robby is settled."

"How long have you been out of work?"

"Hey, man, it's none of your business. I've been getting by, okay? Now drop it."

Certain now that he was on the right track, Luke shook his head. "I don't think so. You see, it seems to me a man who's been out of work for a while might get desperate. He might do something that would never otherwise occur to him."

Tommy's shoulders stiffened. "Such as?"

"Maybe filing a custody suit he had no intention of winning, hoping to get a little cash so he could start over somewhere new." He reached for Tommy's shoulder, clasped it with a firm grip and forced him to turn around. "Is that what the suit was about?"

Suddenly Tommy looked about seventeen again, young and scared and proud. His chin lifted belligerently. "I don't want your money," he declared.

Luke sighed. "Oh, I can believe that. I worked damned hard to instill that streak of stubborn pride in you. That doesn't mean you don't need money, though."

"I'll do just fine once I get to Alaska," Tommy insisted.

Luke carefully weighed the pros and cons before he said anything more. He didn't want to make a mistake that could cost them all. But this was his brother and, as Katie had known, despite everything he loved him unconditionally. Even as angry and as threatened as he'd felt these past months, a part of him had struggled to find an explanation that would make Tommy's betrayal less painful. He still wanted to believe there was something worth salvaging.

Tommy was barely twenty-five. His whole life stretched out in front of him. Maybe all he needed was a solid push in the right direction.

Finally he said, "You could work for me." When Tommy immediately started to object, Luke added, "Just to get the stake you need, if that's the way you want it."

"Bad idea," Tommy said without giving the proposal any thought at all.

"Don't reject it just because of your stupid pride," Luke warned. "At least think about it."

"There's nothing to think about. You don't want me around my kid, and I don't want to be anyplace I'm not wanted. As soon as the judge makes his ruling, I'll take my kid and go." He glared at Luke. "I don't need handouts from you. I don't need anything from you."

Luke didn't believe him. He realized he had started to see him through Katie's eyes, and what he saw was a young man desperate for a sense of belonging. "So why are you here now?"

"You mean tonight? Because Katie invited me." He grinned faintly. "Twisted my arm was more like it."

"Yeah, I know the feeling," Luke commiserated. "But I meant why did you come back to Clover in the first place? The custody suit is being handled in Atlanta. You didn't need to come all the way to South Carolina."

"I wanted to see my son," he insisted.

"You knew I wouldn't let that happen, not under the circumstances."

Tommy shrugged. "I figured you might change your mind."

If he hadn't been so frustrated, he might have laughed at Tommy's stubborn refusal to admit what had been obvious even to Katie. Tommy had come home to be with family. Luke could see that as plainly now as if his brother had scrawled it in a note and posted it in the town square.

But until Tommy could admit he needed help, until he could accept what Luke was willing to offer, there didn't seem to be much Luke could do for him. He'd opened a door tonight, but Tommy had to walk through it.

Fortunately, before his frustration caused him to say something that would set them back, Katie emerged from the house with a platter of hamburgers. She put it down on the picnic table, then lifted her gaze to survey the two of them.

"Everything okay out here?" she asked, regarding them hopefully.

"Terrific," Tommy said with a forced note in his voice.

"Terrific," Luke echoed.

Katie looked pleased. "Well, that's . . . terrific. I'll be out in a minute with the rest of the food. Is the fire hot yet?"

"The coals are glowing like a lover's eyes," Tommy said.

Used to Tommy's tendency to talk explicitly when it came to women, Luke shot him a dark look, but Katie only seemed amused by the response.

"I've never heard anyone get poetic about charcoal before," she said.

To Luke's amazement, Tommy looked faintly sheepish. "Seems like I have a turn of phrase for every occasion."

Katie seemed to forget all about the food that was still waiting inside. She observed Tommy speculatively. "Maybe you should be writing country songs," she said, clearly warming to the possibility.

Luke regarded her with astonishment. "Why the devil would you leap to a conclusion like that?"

"Because he's obviously got a flair with words," she said. "What about it, Tommy? Have you ever thought about it?"

"I've done a couple," Tommy admitted, drawing a smug I-told-you-so look from Katie. "Haven't sold 'em, though. Everybody tells me I'd be a fool to just put 'em in the mail to some singer I don't even know.

Like as not, they'd just steal the song and there wouldn't be nothing I could do about it.''

While Luke stared open-mouthed at his brother, Katie said, ''I'm sure there must be ways to protect yourself. Maybe Luke can help.'' With that less-than-subtle hint, she turned around and sashayed back inside. Luke watched the sway of her hips for a minute, then turned back to his brother.

''Do you really want to write country songs?''

Tommy avoided his gaze. ''Like I said, there's not much chance of selling anything. It's more like a hobby, I guess.''

''But you enjoy it?'' Luke persisted.

''Yeah,'' he admitted, shifting uncomfortably. ''It helps to get stuff out of your system. Sometimes I just have to get what I'm feeling down on paper.''

Luke regarded him with exasperation. ''If writing music is what you want to do, why on earth are you talking about going to Alaska?''

''Because Alaska's more practical. Isn't that the sort of thing you were always preaching to me?''

''Practicality definitely has its place,'' Luke agreed. He turned his gaze on the screen door through which Katie had just disappeared. ''Sometimes, though, you just have to follow your heart.''

Tommy followed the direction of his gaze. ''Is that what brought you back to Clover?'' Tommy asked with a surprising perceptiveness. ''Were you following your heart?''

Maybe because there were protective shadows now that dusk had fallen, maybe because he was feeling more mellow than he had in some time, maybe just because he wanted someone to whom he could admit the truth, Luke said honestly, "I'm beginning to think that is exactly why I came back."

Tommy chuckled. The low sound conveyed more than amusement. To Luke there also seemed to be a note of genuine affection behind it, a hint of understanding.

"What's so funny?" he asked his brother.

"It's just that it's about time you wised up. Everybody always thought you were the smart one, but it always seemed to me that when it came to your feelings for Katie, you were dumber than grass."

Luke laughed. "Now that's a hook for a country song, if ever I heard one."

Something had changed. Katie knew it the minute she walked back outside with the rest of their dinner and heard her husband and Tommy singing enthusiastically. Luke was wildly off-key, but Tommy had a deep, rich voice that was surprisingly sensual and definitely deserved a try at Nashville.

Of course, they were singing some improbable lyric she'd never heard before. It sounded something like, "When it comes to love, I've always been dumber than grass."

"No, no," Tommy protested. "There's no rhyme. It should be, When it comes to love, alas, I've always been dumber than grass."

"Maybe Nashville is beyond your reach, after all," Katie said to Tommy as she joined them.

"I don't know. I was thinking maybe we'd make a good duo," Luke said.

Katie lifted her eyebrows. "I'd think again, if I were you."

Luke slipped an arm around her waist. "If I stay here, will you make it worth my while?"

Luke's touch and the teasing banter shimmered through Katie, reminding her of the intimacy they'd shared just before Tommy's arrival. "What would you consider worth your while?" she inquired, daring to look into eyes that had promptly darkened with desire.

Luke glanced toward an upstairs window. It was probably Mrs. Jeffers' room, but she got the idea.

"Play your cards right and we'll see," she said, then turned to Tommy. "Are those hamburgers done yet? I'm starving."

"Me, too," Luke said, but he wasn't looking toward the grill when he said it. His gaze was pinned directly on her.

The banter and easy camaraderie lasted through dinner. Luke seemed to have let down his guard with his brother, and Tommy's belligerence disappeared. As soon as the dishes had been cleared, all three of them by some unspoken agreement went back outside into the soft night air, where the only thing breaking the silence was the sound of crickets chirping. Lightning bugs flickered against the velvet darkness.

As if he sensed—or hoped, at least—that she wouldn't refuse, Luke took Katie's hand and led her to the hammock that was strung between two sturdy oak trees. He climbed in, then tugged her in alongside him. She went into his arms without resisting and settled her head on his shoulder.

Tommy cleared his throat and remained standing. "Maybe I should be taking off."

Katie started to protest, but Luke sent his brother a grateful look.

"Stop by the office in the morning," Luke said. "We'll talk some more."

"I told you before..." Tommy began, a belligerent note creeping back into his voice.

Katie jumped in. "There's no harm in talking, is there, Tommy?"

"Damn, but you're pushy, Katie," he accused, but there was a lightness in his voice that hadn't been there before tonight. "Seems to me you and my brother are about evenly matched."

"Does that mean you'll show up?" she asked.

"I'll show up," he said. Suddenly he grinned at the two of them sprawled practically on top of each other in the hammock. "You two have a good evening."

"You, too," Luke said quietly.

Only after Tommy had gone did he add, "I wonder where the hell he's staying."

"He didn't tell you?"

"Not a word. I don't think he's got a dime to his name, either." He sighed heavily, and his arms around Katie tightened. "I think you may have been right. I think he's been down on his luck for a long time now and wanted to come home. Robby gave him the excuse he needed."

Though she was increasingly aware of Luke's body pressed intimately against her own, Katie tried to keep her attention focused on loftier things. If she wouldn't let Luke into her bedroom, she'd be damned if she was going to make love with him in a hammock. That would certainly violate the spirit, if not the letter of their contract.

"Are you planning to offer him work?" she asked, trying to ignore the sweep of Luke's hand from hip to thigh and back again.

"I did. And he told me to take my job and, well you know the rest."

"Can't you find some way to help him get a break in Nashville?"

"Katie, you heard us singing. Did those lyrics sound as if they stand a chance of climbing the country music charts?"

"How long did it take him to write them?"

"About ten seconds, but that's not the point."

"It is the point," she corrected. "If he can do that in ten seconds, just think what he could do if he actually worked at it. Besides, he has an incredible voice and the kind of bad-boy looks that could make him a star."

Luke stared at her. "You're serious, aren't you?"

"Dead serious. If you think I'm wrong, get him a gig closer to home and check it out. He could probably work some club in Myrtle Beach. Country music is everywhere up there."

She gazed into blue eyes that were suddenly thoughtful and added, "Besides, if Tommy finds a place for himself, if he's doing something he loves, I don't think he'll press for custody of Robby. You can end this before it ever gets to court."

Luke cupped her face in his hands. "Have I mentioned that I love you, Katie Cassidy?"

The impulsive statement sent shock waves rebounding through her. Of course, she knew he didn't mean it. Not in any way that counted. He was just grateful for the mediating she'd done that had eased tensions between him and his brother. That was all it was, she told herself sternly right before Luke's mouth settled against hers in the sweetest, gentlest kiss she'd ever experienced.

On the surface there was nothing provocative or even remotely dangerous about that kiss, but Katie's body apparently didn't know that. She responded as if it were the darkest, most sensual, most seductive invitation ever delivered. And she knew without a doubt, as her pulse scrambled and her heart thundered, that she was within seconds of losing the last fragile thread of her resolve.

It took her only one of those scant remaining seconds to bolt from the hammock, practically toppling Luke onto the ground with her.

"What the . . . ?" Luke demanded, looking dazed.

"I'm going to bed," Katie announced with as much dignity as she could muster.

"Good. I'll—" Luke began, apparently taking her words as an invitation.

She frowned at him. "I'll see you in the morning."

He halted where he was. "I see."

He looked so taken aback, so thoroughly confused by her sudden change that Katie almost took pity on him . . . and herself. Only a reminder that Luke had chosen her not as a wife, but as a means to an end kept her from throwing herself back into his arms.

"I'll be at the diner by the time you get up," she said in a tone designed to put as much emotional distance back between them as possible. "Peg will probably have Robby there by then, too. If you come by..." she gazed into stormy eyes "...I'll take a break and we can all have breakfast together."

Luke looked as if he were about to protest, but finally he shook his head and turned away.

"We had a deal," Katie reminded him softly.

"I don't want to hear another word about the damned deal," he said. "Just go to bed, Katie. Go now, unless you want me to prove that you want to tear up that blasted paper even more than I do."

He was right, she thought. If she stayed, there would be no turning back, and she wasn't ready to risk it yet. She cast one last tormented look in Luke's direction, then turned and went inside. One irony did not escape her. She had smoothed over Luke's relationship with his brother, but his relationship with her was in more turmoil than ever.

Chapter Twelve

Luke didn't show up at the diner. Katie watched for him all morning long, delaying her break until she was practically faint with hunger. Robby had long since protested the delay and demanded pancakes with an egg on top "the way Daddy likes." Once he'd eaten, he couldn't wait to go off with Mrs. Jeffers, who was beginning to look a little frazzled, but who swore she was having more fun than she'd had in years.

At the door to the diner, Mrs. Jeffers turned and came back. "Dear, I don't want you worrying about what happened yesterday," she said, squeezing Katie's hand reassuringly. "Luke is absolutely right about the rent. We've all been taking advantage of your good nature. I'm sure we'll manage to get on the proper schedule somehow."

Katie stared at her, feeling her temper start to rise all over again. Everyone was just assuming again that Luke was in charge. "The schedule you were on was just fine," she said tightly. "There is no need for any of you to be upset. I'll handle Luke."

Mrs. Jeffers looked alarmed by her anger. "Now, Katie, don't you dare start fighting with your new husband over this. This should be a time of joy for the two of you. Like I said, we'll manage."

"And like I said, there's no need for anyone to manage anything. You'll pay me just as you always have and that's the end of it."

"If you say so, dear," Mrs. Jeffers said doubtfully. She started toward the door, then turned back again. "One last thing, should I bring Robby back to the boarding house after our outing or take him to Peg's?"

"Bring him to the boarding house," Katie said, suddenly reaching a decision she should have made the moment she and Luke returned from Atlanta. If they were ever going to have anything resembling a normal marriage or even a decent business partnership, then they needed to get everyone back under one roof so they could all adjust together. "I think it's time everyone came home where they belonged. I'll expect to see you and Ginger and Mr. O'Reilly there tonight, as well."

The pleased expression on Mrs. Jeffers's face indicated to Katie that the woman had no idea she was part of a gauntlet being thrown down in front of Luke.

Katie was still formulating her strategy for showing Luke once and for all that he did not control the running of the boarding house, when Ginger pulled her aside.

"I heard what you said to Mrs. Jeffers," Ginger said, her voice shaking. "Do you really think you can convince Luke to back down?" Tears formed in her eyes. "I don't want to have to leave, Katie. The boarding house is home to me."

"And it will stay your home," Katie said, biting back the first sharp retort that had come to mind. "It's my boarding house. I set the rules."

"But Luke..."

"Luke may understand big business, but he doesn't know a darn thing about *my* business," Katie snapped. "I think it's time we cleared that up."

"But he told me that if I didn't pay my rent, he would evict me."

Katie saw red. "He told you that?" she said incredulously. "He actually used those words?"

Ginger nodded. "He as much as said it before you showed up yesterday. It's not like I don't see his point," she whispered, choking back a sob. "I really do, but Katie, you told me school was important. You made me see that. I can't go to school and work a full-time job to pay the rent. The hours here are about all I can manage and I'm putting that money away for college."

"Stop worrying about it. You're doing exactly what I want you to do. I'll settle this with Luke."

Ginger didn't look particularly reassured by Katie's declaration. If anything, she looked even more concerned, but whatever doubts she had she kept to herself.

Amazingly enough, so did Peg, who had come through the swinging door just in time to hear most of the conversation. Other than the inscrutable expression on her face, she might have been deaf to the obvious storm her niece intended to stir up. Katie was grateful that for once her aunt intended to let her handle her own problems.

Mr. O'Reilly, however, wasn't nearly so reticent. He caught Katie on the front porch when she returned to the boarding house later that afternoon.

"I think it's time we had a talk," he said, indicating the rocking chair next to him.

Katie sank into it gratefully. After more than six hours on her feet, she was ready to sit down. She looked over at the retired fireman, whose expression was combative, and realized this wasn't going to be one of the friendly little chats they usually had in the afternoon. She suspected there would be no anecdotes about his heroics as a fireman in Charleston and probably not even the lecture on fire safety that she'd come to expect. The man turned positively rapturous over smoke alarms. He'd personally seen to it that the boarding house had the most technologically advanced ones on the market and he'd done it at his own expense.

"What's the problem?" she asked.

"Too many rules."

"What rules?" she inquired warily.

"These rules," he said, waving a sheet of bright canary yellow paper in front of her. "I found it under my door when I got back to my room earlier. Then your husband made it a point to let me know that he planned to enforce each and every one of them."

With a sinking sensation in the pit of her stomach, Katie reluctantly accepted the piece of paper. "Rules of the Clover Street Boarding House" headed the page. First on the list was the deadline for paying rent, with appropriate penalties for late payment. That was followed by a schedule for using the downstairs rooms that included a 10:00 p.m. curfew on weeknights, 11:00 p.m. on weekends. There were more, but when she came to rule number nine, Katie knew she'd hit on the one that Mr. O'Reilly was most upset about.

"No boarder may raid the refrigerator for between-meal snacks."

Katie groaned. What the dickens had Luke been thinking of? If he had his way, the boarding house would soon seem no friendlier than a prison. She balled the paper into a wad and said, "I'll handle this."

Mr. O'Reilly's disgruntled expression suggested he didn't have a lot of faith in her handling her husband. "If you can't," he warned, "I'll be moving out at the end of the week. Life's too short to be staying where I'm not wanted."

"Nobody will be moving out," Katie promised. Unless it was her new husband, she amended, and she might very well be chasing him out with a broom.

Katie couldn't find any sign of Luke anywhere in the house. All she found were more of those damnable colored sheets of paper, posted everywhere and shoved under every door. He'd probably placed an ad in the Clover weekly as well.

She hunted through the pile of papers on her desk until she found his new business card with the office number on it. She dialed, tapping her foot impatiently as she waited for him to pick up. When he finally did, she heard the unexpected sound of a guitar accompanying Tommy's unmistakable, sexy voice. If she hadn't been quite so furious, that might have silenced her.

Instead she said in a slow, measured voice, "Get home now, Luke Cassidy, or I won't be responsible for what you find when you get here."

Before he could say one way or the other whether he would come, she slammed the phone back into its cradle.

Luke winced as the sound of the crashing phone reverberated in his ear. Tommy must have caught his reaction, because he stopped strumming his guitar and regarded Luke worriedly.

"Everything okay?"

"Katie seems anxious to see me at home," he said in what had to be the most massive understatement he'd ever uttered. He'd never heard that particular tone of command in her voice before. He found it exhilarating... and perhaps just the slightest bit worrisome.

Tommy grinned. "Well, well, things must be heating up."

"You could say that," Luke said dryly. "Look, I'd better run. We'll talk more about this music career you want later. Give me a call tonight."

Tommy's knowing smile broadened. "Maybe I'll wait till morning, big brother. Your mood should be real mellow by then."

Luke decided to let him have his illusions. One of them might as well get some pleasure from anticipating the evening's prospects. He, unfortunately, knew better than to expect that a welcome mat was being tossed down for him.

As he walked home, he realized his timing in writing that memo to the boarding house residents might have been just a little off. Katie was putting a lot of energy into this campaign to salvage his relationship with his brother and to stave off a court battle for custody of Robby. She hadn't yet adapted to being married, though she seemed to be getting into the spirit of being a mother. She definitely wasn't quite ready to adjust to the idea that now she had someone to look out for her best interests.

Nor had she accepted that their bargain gave him some measure of control over the operation of the boarding house. Luke was willing to admit that maybe he'd been a little heavy-handed about trying to take over the financial end of things. But Katie needed to learn that she couldn't keep letting the boarding house residents pay her if and when they got around to it. He had to stop all the other ways the boarders took advantage of her as well.

Yes, indeed, he knew in his gut that he'd made the right decision in drawing up those rules. His biggest mistake had probably been talking to the tenants directly and posting the notices before mentioning them to Katie. He already knew how testy she could get about anyone trying to usurp her power around the place. She hadn't exactly welcomed his past efforts.

He found her waiting for him on the front porch, a glass of lemonade in hand that was probably only slightly more sour than her apparent mood. She did not smile when she saw him. She continued to push herself lazily back and forth in the swing as if she were trying to stir up a breeze. Her hair had been scooped up and tied with a scarf. She was wearing an old pair of cutoff jeans and a tank top. Her feet were bare. She hadn't even bothered with lipstick. She looked ... entrancing.

And very, very angry, he decided with some dismay, but no surprise.

Sucking in a deep breath, Luke brazenly plunked himself into the swing next to her. She was apparently too tired to protest or to move.

"Just how mad are you?" he asked eventually.

"Mad enough."

He decided to go straight to the heart of the situation. "Do you want out of our deal?" he asked. Even as the words came out of his mouth, he realized that that thought had been behind his precipitous actions. In some weird way, he'd been testing her, hoping to discover if she would choose him over the boarding house.

His blunt question drew a startled look. "Do you?"

"No," he admitted, though he was unwilling to elaborate on just what he did want. He wasn't even sure he could put it into words or, more precisely, that he was willing to.

Katie sighed. "Neither do I." She was quiet for a long time. When she finally spoke up, she surprised him by saying, "It's not the way I imagined it would be."

"What?"

"Marriage."

"In general or to me?" It was the first time he'd even considered the possibility that she had ever cared for him enough to marry him for all the traditional reasons, rather than the trumped up business deal they'd settled for instead.

"Both, I suppose."

"That's because we're not sleeping together," he suggested, seizing the most obvious explanation he could think of—and the most convenient, given his own increasingly demanding goal. He would have seduced her right here, right now, if he weren't certain he'd get a fist in his solar plexus for his efforts.

Katie shook her head. Something in her eyes told him she pitied him.

"You really don't have a clue, do you?" she asked.

"About what?"

She sighed again. "Never mind."

Luke dared for the first time to touch the strand of hair that had escaped from her saucy ponytail. He brushed it back from her cheek, his knuckles skimming along skin that felt like satin. A thousand memories stole through him, a thousand sensations from the one night they had made love so long ago.

Was it possible that those were the memories that had drawn him back to Clover? Was it the promised joy of loving Katie that had lured him home, rather than the practical need to solve some legal dilemma that had turned his life upside down? Tommy certainly seemed to think so. He'd even begun to suspect it himself. But how would he ever know for sure? And would it even matter, if he could figure it out?

What had happened to her life, Katie wondered with a sense of desperation as she struggled to ignore the sensations Luke's casual, but persistent touch was stirring inside her. A few months ago, she had been leading a quiet, peaceful existence. She had successfully—well, almost successfully—driven Luke Cassidy from her mind. She was operating a business she loved, surrounded by people she cared about. Life hadn't been perfect, but she'd been content.

She hadn't even minded so very much that it seemed she was destined to be always a bridesmaid, but never a bride. All those couples—Hannah and Matthew, Emma and Michael, Sophie and Ford and especially Lucy and Max—were family. There would be lots of babies for her to love. Lots of people were not nearly so blessed.

Now her entire household was in an uproar because of the endless regulations Luke had instituted. And on Friday Henrietta Myers would be moving in, which gave Katie plenty to complain about herself.

Where was she supposed to put Luke? She knew perfectly well that he intended to make himself at home in her room. She also knew that her resistance was just about taxed to the limit as it was. If the man climbed into her bed, if he so much as brushed against her during the night, she didn't have a prayer of staying out of his arms. There was so much heat between them lately, if they were caught in the rain these days they would send up steam.

It seemed to her that that risk was far more dangerous than the prospect of losing her current boarders. She could find new boarders, if she had to. Ginger, Mr. O'Reilly and the others could find adequate accommodations elsewhere, if necessary. But she absolutely could not live with the consequences of making love with Luke knowing that he wasn't in love with her, knowing that she was merely convenient, rather than the grand passion of his life as he was of hers.

If she was going to take charge of her life again, if she was going to protect herself and her boarders, then she had no choice. She had to remind Luke that this arrangement they had did not include his bullying tactics. Besides, if things worked out with Robby's custody, for all she knew he would take off. The disruptions would have been pointless, because she would never enforce them on her own.

When she could delay it no longer, she turned to face him. "I don't like what you're doing around here," she said bluntly, waving the sheet of canary yellow paper under his nose.

Luke stiffened. His hand fell away from her shoulder as if he'd been scalded. The faint teasing glint in his eyes faded as his expression immediately turned somber.

"I know I should have talked to you first," he admitted. "But I know how you are. You would have tried to talk me out of those rules."

"Damn right, I would have. The disruptions around here have gotten out of hand," she said, perversely wishing she could tease his lips back into a smile. She barely resisted the temptation to try, to run the tip of her finger along the velvet skin of his lower lip to encourage it into an upward curve. Touching him right now would be a very bad idea. Very bad.

"Our deal put me in charge of the financial end of running the boarding house," he reminded her.

"It put me in charge of dealing with the tenants," she retorted. "As it is, Ginger's terrified you're going to evict her. Where would she get an idea like that?"

"I had a talk with her," he admitted. "I thought she should understand that we're running a business. I hope you didn't undermine the message I was trying to get across."

Katie scowled at him. "I'm sure that's how you would see it. I told her we would never evict her."

"She's never paid one cent of rent," Luke pointed out in that calm, reasonable way that made Katie want to grind her teeth. "I went back over the books for all the months she's been here."

"She's seventeen years old. It's more important that she stay off the streets of some big city and finish school. Besides, she helps me out around here."

Luke shot her a look of total disbelief. "Doing what?"

Katie had to be quick on her feet to answer that one, especially since Ginger hadn't even been around since she had gone to work at the diner. "She changes the beds, helps with the laundry, straightens up, vacuums, those kinds of things," she said, blithely ignoring the fact that Ginger probably didn't even have a clue where the cleaning supplies were kept.

"If she does all that, why do I see you changing sheets, doing tub after tub of laundry and shoving a vacuum around?"

Katie winced. "I said she helps. I didn't say she did everything. If I paid her a wage, it would more than make up for what she would have to pay for the room. I'm coming out ahead on the deal."

"Then let's make her a part-time employee," Luke countered. "That way she'll have very specific responsibilities and she'll be able to pay her own way."

"What good does it do to give her money and have her give it right back to us? That's just a bunch of paperwork."

"It'll teach her responsibility," Luke insisted.

Katie tried to make him see reason. "She doesn't need to feel responsible," she said impatiently. "She needs to feel like she's part of a family."

That silenced him.

Taking advantage of that, Katie plunged on. "Now about Mr. O'Reilly. You talked to him, too, didn't you? You didn't just hand him that piece of paper."

"We had a chat over coffee this morning, yes."

"A chat? Is that what you call it when you declare that the kitchen is off-limits between meals?"

"But..."

Katie ignored him. "How much can an occasional midnight snack cost? Besides, it—"

"Let me guess," Luke said resignedly. "It makes him feel like he's part of a family."

Katie beamed at him. Maybe he was catching on, after all. "Exactly," she said, pleased.

He studied her intently. "Do you know what would make me feel like part of a family?"

There was something in his voice that set Katie's senses on fire. Her gaze locked with his. The intensity burning between them made her tremble. "What?"

"Sharing your bed."

She couldn't seem to catch her breath. "Oh, no..." she began in a choked voice. The rest of the protest died on her lips when he pressed a silencing finger against them.

As if he sensed she was weakening, he coaxed, "I'm your husband. That's where I belong. You wouldn't want me to feel like an outsider in my own home, would you?"

"No, but..."

He lowered his head until his lips hovered over hers, so close his minty breath fanned her hot skin and his purely masculine scent surrounded her. Katie's breath snagged in her throat. When his mouth finally settled on hers, the whole world tilted on its axis. Suddenly it was impossible to recall what they were arguing about, impossible to think of anything except the indescribable way she felt when Luke touched her.

"Not fair," she murmured eventually. Her arms seemed to have twined themselves around his neck of their own free will. She couldn't find the resolve to remove them.

"I don't recall any mention of *fair* in the wedding vows," Luke said, a surprising twinkle appearing in his eyes. That spark chased away the last of the shadows. "I do seem to recall an expression that all's fair in love and war."

His expression suddenly sobered. "I want a real marriage, Katie, in every way."

Love? A real marriage? Her heart pounded ecstatically. Katie studied Luke's face to see if he realized what he'd said. Or was it one more example of words slipping out with no substance behind them? Just a convenient ploy to lure her into his bed?

Then, again, could it possibly be true that he loved her half as much as she loved him? His enigmatic expression told her nothing. Maybe this was something she was going to have to take on faith. Maybe it required a giant-size risk. She was already in this relationship up to her neck, anyway.

"You can move into our room on Friday, when Mrs. Myers gets here."

"Tonight," he argued, evidently not satisfied with the hard-won victory. He sprinkled more persuasive kisses across her brow and onto her cheeks.

"You're pushing it, Cassidy," she said without much oomph behind the protest.

"I'm desperate," he admitted in a way that gave her goose bumps. "Besides, how else will I know you're not just letting me in because my room is rented?"

His kisses deepened, leaving Katie breathless, her senses reeling.

"Tonight," she agreed eventually, because if anything, she wanted him in her bed even more desperately than he wanted to be there. Fighting it any longer seemed likely to be an exercise in futility.

"Tonight," she repeated in a whisper that only hinted at the deep, unspoken yearning in her heart. It would either be the best decision she had ever made . . . or the worst.

Chapter Thirteen

There were too damned many people living in the
boarding house, Luke decided about nine o'clock. He
and Katie were still surrounded by boarders, to say
nothing of his son who was too excited about finally
living in his new home "for real" to go off to bed. If
Luke hadn't recognized that it would be opening yet
another major can of worms, he would have ordered
every one of them back to the Clover Street Hotel so
he and Katie could have some privacy.

It was another nerve-racking hour before they all
finally began drifting off to their own rooms. Alone
with Katie at last, Luke met her gaze and saw a riot of
emotions burning in the emerald depths of her eyes.
He was sure his own eyes mirrored that same sort of
turbulence. He'd been aching for her ever since she'd

agreed to let him move into their room that night. Longer, actually. He could trace this hunger back to the first day he'd seen her after his return to Clover.

"Ready?" he asked, holding out his hand.

Gazing at him solemnly, she stood and came slowly toward him. He couldn't miss her nervous, hard swallow, or the faint trembling as she placed her hand in his.

"Scared?" he asked, surprised.

"Of you?" she said. "Never."

He found the touch of defiance in her voice amusing. "Of us, then?"

She struggled visibly with her answer before admitting what he could already read in her eyes. "A little. It's been a long time, Luke."

"Too long," he agreed softly, his gaze locked with hers. "Far too long." He felt a smile tugging at his lips. "For the first time, I actually feel like a newlywed." Because he wanted her to understand that he was referring not just to their recent wedding, but to the past, he added, "For the first time *ever*."

Color bloomed in Katie's cheeks. "Me, too," she said with a touching shyness.

Suddenly he couldn't bear to wait a moment longer. He scooped her into his arms and headed for the stairs.

"Luke, what on earth are you doing?" she demanded, laughing.

"It's tradition," he reminded her.

"But you've already carried me across the threshold once."

''That was for show,'' he said. ''This time it's just the two of us. Tonight's the night our marriage really begins.''

With a soft little sigh, Katie settled against his chest. An emotion more powerful than anything he'd ever experienced rushed through him. Tenderness, yearning and something that even his jaded heart recognized as love filled him.

Oh, he knew there were doubts to overcome, hers and his. He knew there were obstacles in their path, not the least of which was the impending custody battle. But suddenly, with every fiber of his being, he recognized that this was where he wanted to be, where he belonged.

And the woman in his arms was the only one he would ever love. Years ago he'd fallen in love with a girl. Today Katie was all grown up, a woman of strength and beauty and generosity. Those qualities had always been there, but they'd matured.

Today Caitlyn Jones Cassidy was a spirited force to be reckoned with. And she was his, legally anyway... as long as he didn't do something stupid and blow it. Tonight was his chance to cement their relationship. Otherwise he feared that when Robby's custody was finally settled, when she had lived up to that part of their bargain, Katie could very well walk away. He knew that if she did his life would never be the same.

When Luke had nudged open the door to her room, Katie gasped in amazement. He'd filled the room with flowers—bright, splashy, fragrant flowers. The ceiling fan created a deliciously scented breeze. A bottle of champagne was on ice in an elegant silver bucket.

And somehow he had found the filmy negligee that had been meant for her wedding night. It had been shoved in the back of a dresser drawer, behind over-size T-shirts and warm flannel gowns. At the thought of Luke's hands sorting through her things, a delight-ful heat began to spread slowly through her. Just the sight of that pale chiffon, shimmering against the bed's dark green comforter, warmed her.

"You've been busy," she observed, looking into eyes filled with anticipation and blatant masculine desire, rather than the smug satisfaction she might have expected under the circumstances.

"I thought this called for a celebration," he said.

"Do you intend to celebrate like this whenever you get your way?" she asked, unable to resist the tart question.

"If I do, will you give in more often?"

She grinned at the teasing note in his voice. "I wouldn't count on it."

"Somehow I thought that would be your answer," he said, sounding surprisingly pleased. He held up the negligee. "Want some privacy while you change into this?"

She snatched it from his hand and headed for the adjoining bathroom.

"Don't take too long," he pleaded in a voice that had grown husky.

"You can keep busy opening the champagne," she said, wishing she had a glass to take along with her.

She wasn't sure where she'd get the nerve to emerge from the bathroom in that revealing gown without it.

She recognized as soon as she'd closed the door behind her that she would collapse with a bad case of stage fright if she didn't hurry. She was all thumbs as it was as she stripped off her clothes, took a hurried shower, then pulled the filmy gown on. She stood in front of the steamy mirror and marveled at what she saw.

There was a faint hint of curl in her tousled hair. Her cheeks were bright with becoming color. Her eyes were sparkling with anticipation. She looked . . . like a bride, every bit as radiant as the picture-perfect bride Peg had described for her with such longing. Dear heaven, she told herself with a sense of amazement, after what seemed to be an eternity of waiting, she really was about to be a bride in more than name only. Luke's bride.

Drawing in a deep, trembling breath, she finally opened the door. She had to cling to the frame for support when she saw Luke standing at the window, wearing only his dark trousers. The well-defined muscles in his shoulders and back seemed to beckon for her touch. His skin was more bronzed now than it had been when he'd first arrived back in Clover. He looked even more breathtakingly masculine than he had six years ago.

Yet she knew exactly how he would feel if she stroked her fingers over his bare flesh. The skin would be supple, and it would burn wherever she dared to caress. She absorbed all of this in the space of a heartbeat.

At the sound of the door opening, he turned, facing her, his expression avid as his gaze swept over her. The hunger and electricity charging that gaze could have lit up the entire town of Clover, maybe the entire state of South Carolina.

Since Katie couldn't seem to move, he picked up the two flutes of champagne and came slowly toward her. She accepted the glass. Her pulse skittered wildly as their fingers brushed.

"You look...breathtaking," he said in a voice that had turned low and seductive.

"I feel..." Katie found she couldn't begin to describe the sensations rippling through her. She felt slightly breathless, slightly anxious and deliciously aroused all at once.

Luke carefully set his glass down and reached for her. "You feel," he began, turning her words around and filling in the space she'd left blank, "like fire and silk."

His fingers skimmed along her arms, leaving heat in their wake. That same delicate stroking over sheer chiffon made her skin tingle with shivery awareness. Her nipples hardened at once, responding to the repeated return of tormenting touches. When he lowered his head and took one sensitive, thinly covered peak into his mouth, she shuddered, reaching for his bare shoulders and clinging just to remain upright.

The sensation was exquisite, sweeter than she'd recalled in her wildest memories of that other time, that other tender claiming.

Unfortunately, rather than adding to the provocative sensations Luke was stirring in her now, the memories suddenly cooled her ardor. Oh, her body was his, responding to his touches with predictable abandon. She couldn't have prevented that if she'd tried. She'd waited far too long for this moment.

But her heart withdrew into a protective shell. Even as Luke entered her with a slow, thrilling stroke that filled her and lured her toward an explosive release, somewhere deep inside she remained aloof and terrified.

Terrified that once again their love was an illusion, that once again it wouldn't last.

And when Luke saw the silent tears spilling down her cheeks, when he asked what was wrong in a voice that shook with concern, Katie couldn't answer. She simply wrapped her arms around him and held on for dear life, hoping that somehow, some way she would never have to let go.

Ironically, after all his sneaky conniving to make it happen, Luke found that making love to Katie was bittersweet. As perfectly attuned as they had been in bed, as sweetly erotic and wickedly demanding as the night had been, something had been missing. Something had gone terribly wrong, leaving Katie in tears she couldn't—or wouldn't—explain.

A few weeks ago, absorbed with his single-minded pursuit of marriage, not love, he probably wouldn't have noticed the lack at all, but now he recognized it for what it surely had to be. Katie had made love with him, but she wasn't *in love* with him. She had held something back, some essential part of herself.

Sitting in the kitchen at dawn, drinking a cup of coffee, he couldn't help thinking about the first time they had made love. Katie had been totally inexperienced. He had been young and anxious. But love had made every touch magic, every kiss joyous. There had been no holding back for either of them.

Last night, with Katie asleep in his arms, he'd felt a fleeting sense of triumph. This morning, after hours of lying awake analyzing it, he realized that it had been a shallow victory. Katie had shared her body, but not her heart. He wondered bleakly if he would ever get that back again.

It all came back to this damned bargain they'd struck. He wondered if either of them would ever trust the other's motives as long as their deal remained on the table. Even as they had been lifted to the height of passion, even as she had murmured his name over and over, Luke couldn't help remembering everything that had led to their being together in that bed.

And perversely he couldn't help thinking that if Katie loved him, if she had ever loved him, she would have told him to take a flying leap when he'd suggested this marriage of convenience. She would have held out for the declaration of love and commitment she deserved.

No, the truth of it was that all she wanted from him was a way to save her boarding house and support this surrogate family of hers.

He had thought sex would make him part of Katie's life, part of her family. Instead, it had left him feeling lonelier than ever.

He wondered what would happen when the boarding house's bottom line was in the black and the custody suit was over. Would Katie stick with him or leave? He was more certain than ever that he knew the answer. She would go.

In those gray minutes of first light, he reached a decision. He had gotten them into this mess by thinking only of his own short-term need for a wife and a mother for his son. He would get them out again by focusing on what he really needed, Katie's love.

It shouldn't take more than what? A little ingenuity? He was acclaimed for that. A little determination? The word mule-headed had been applied to him more than once. And a lifetime of knowing Katie? There was no one on earth who knew her better.

To accomplish a miracle, though, he needed time. More time than the wheels of justice he'd oiled would give him. With that in mind, he called his attorney, oblivious to the fact that he might be waking Andrew Lawton from a sound sleep. But Andrew had disrupted his share of Luke's nights when he'd been going through his own very messy divorce.

"When are we due to go to court for the custody ruling?" Luke asked without even a "good morning" for the man he'd first met within weeks after he'd arrived in Atlanta. They'd been friends ever since, as well as business associates.

"Luke, what the devil..." Andrew muttered, sounding both sleepy and disgruntled.

Luke repeated his question.

"It's on the judge's calendar for the end of the month. It could be anytime that last week in June,"

Andrew told him, sounding considerably more alert once he grasped that this wasn't just idle curiosity on Luke's part. "Tommy's lawyer has been pressing to have it moved up, though. He agrees with us that for Robby's sake this needs to be concluded as quickly as possible."

It was exactly as Luke had feared. His time with Katie was running out. "Delay it," Luke said.

There was a lengthy silence before Andrew responded. "I thought you wanted to get it over with," he said, sounding confused. "We're prepared. The reports are into the court. Why wait for—?"

Luke cut in. "I want you to drag this out as long as possible."

"Luke, you're not making any sense," Andrew protested. "Just last week..."

"I don't give a damn what I said last week."

"Okay, what's going on?" Andrew asked quietly. "You and Katie aren't having problems, are you? Do you need time to work them out? If that's the case, the longer we delay, the more likely Tommy will find out about the problem and use it against you."

Luke sighed. "There is no problem, at least not one that I can't solve, if you'll just buy me some time. Please, Andrew, do what you can. Take a vacation. Tell them you've got a case in Tasmania or something. Just get the case delayed."

"I'll do what I can," Andrew agreed finally. "If you need to talk, buddy, let me know."

"I don't need to talk," Luke said curtly and hung up. He turned to find Katie staring at him in openmouthed astonishment.

"I think you do," she said quietly, her gaze cutting straight through him.

"Do what?"

"Need to talk." She poured herself a cup of coffee, seated herself very precisely across from him at the kitchen table and regarded him expectantly. "You can start anytime now. Why would you ask your lawyer to delay the custody case?"

Luke looked everywhere but at his wife. "I just told Andrew that I want to be sure we're fully prepared. This is too important to make mistakes."

"Does Andrew think everything's ready? Is he in the habit of making mistakes?"

"Andrew doesn't know everything, and everyone makes mistakes."

"What is it that your attorney doesn't know?"

The direct question stymied him. He didn't want to admit that he was buying time for the two of them, that he wanted to solidify what they had begun the night before—a real marriage. And there was also the possibility that Katie had been right about Tommy. Perhaps with just a little more time he and his brother could mend fences and Tommy would drop the suit. Time seemed the answer to everything.

"I just think it's for the best," he said finally.

Katie regarded him incredulously. "For whom? What about Robby? Don't you think he's beginning to suspect that something serious is going on? He can't help but feel the tension every time Tommy calls here. Sooner or later he's going to start asking why he hasn't met his uncle. And how much longer do you think you can keep Tommy from barging in and telling him the truth? If you're going to drag this out intentionally, then you'd better sit down with your son and tell him exactly what's happening, before he hears it from your brother.''

"Katie..."

Before he could get out another word, she'd grabbed her cup of coffee and headed out the back door, letting it slam behind her. Luke stared after her.

"Well, that certainly went well," he muttered to himself. At this rate, his damned plan would land them in divorce court.

Katie had no idea what had happened to Luke between the time they went upstairs together and the moment he'd slipped out of bed and abandoned her that morning a few days earlier. No matter how she tried, she couldn't begin to figure out why Luke had placed that call to his attorney.

Over the past few days, though, she had watched in bemusement as Luke seemed to be transformed before her eyes.

She had come home one day to find him tutoring Ginger in math, leading her step by step through a tricky problem with admirable patience. Ginger's head bobbed in understanding as he explained each step. And when she reached the correct answer to the next problem completely on her own, she beamed at Luke with an expression akin to hero worship.

The next night, unable to sleep, Katie had wandered down to the kitchen at midnight and found Mr. O'Reilly and Luke there ahead of her, huge bowls of ice cream in front of them. She stayed back in the

shadows and listened. Mr. O'Reilly was telling Luke
all about the time he'd saved a little girl from a blaze
in the rat-infested basement of a tenement. Katie had
heard the story a dozen times and each time tears had
come to her eyes. Luke seemed equally shaken by the
near tragedy.

"Dear God," he murmured. "Maybe we'd better
take a look through here tomorrow. Make sure all the
alarms are in working order."

"They are," the retired fireman assured him. "I see
to it myself. Nothing like that'll happen to Katie, if
I'm around to prevent it. That girl is like a daughter to
me." He met Luke's gaze. "And that boy of yours,
he's a real pistol. Livens the place up. Mrs. Jeffers is
looking downright young again, now that she has a
little one to do for."

Luke's expression turned speculative. "So you've
noticed what a fine figure of a woman Mrs. Jeffers is."

Red crept into Mr. O'Reilly's cheeks. "Now don't
you go getting any ideas. I'm too old to be carrying
on."

Luke's low laughter warmed Katie's heart.

"You're never too old," he declared.

Pleased more than she could say by the scene she
had stumbled on, Katie had slipped away before either of them saw her.

Just this morning she found a stack of neat little
printed notices on the table where whoever picked up
the mail each day left it for the others. She picked one
up and was stunned when she read that the weekly rent
was being cut by ten percent. She couldn't decide
whether to laugh or cry. Luke had clearly lost his

mind. She'd wanted him to loosen up, but at this rate he would bankrupt her.

With one of the slips in hand, she headed straight down the street to his office. He was leaning back in his fancy new leather chair behind his fancy new mahogany desk, looking pleased as punch about something.

"Are you okay?" she asked straight out.

He grinned. "Better than ever."

She plucked the little white notice from her purse and shoved it across his desk. "Then maybe you can explain what you were thinking when you did this."

"The economy's tight," he explained without batting an eye. "We have to be competitive."

"With whom? There's no place else in town that offers people room and board. And last I heard the manager of the hotel wasn't tutoring his guests in his spare time."

Luke shrugged. "It's no big deal."

"What happened to all that talk about sound fiscal responsibility? Are you trying to bankrupt me?"

"We can afford to absorb a few losses on the boarding house. I have other investments that will more than balance things out."

Katie couldn't believe what she was hearing. "Those are your investments. The boarding house is mine. You promised to get it onto a sound financial footing."

His expression perfectly bland, he said, "Some things are more important than money."

Katie regarded him suspiciously. A statement like that sounded like heresy coming from him. "Such as?"

"Family," he replied quietly.

"Family?" she repeated as if it were a foreign concept. "Luke, what is going on here?"

He leaned forward, his gaze locking with hers. "I have finally figured out what's important in life," he said. "Now I intend to do everything in my power to see that I get it."

If there hadn't been such a note of grim determination in his voice, Katie might have laughed. She recalled the night she'd hauled everyone back to the boarding house as a way of throwing a gauntlet down in front of her husband. It seemed he'd just returned the challenge.

She still wasn't certain exactly what was going on in Luke's head, but she was beginning to grasp one thing. Finally it appeared they were both chasing the same dream.

Chapter Fourteen

"We're going out tonight," Luke announced when he was finally able to snag Katie for a second during the morning rush at Peg's Diner.

There was a spark of mischief in his eyes she hadn't seen since they were teenagers. "Where?"

"You'll see. Just put on your party clothes and be ready by six."

"Who's baby-sitting Robby?"

"Don't worry. It's all taken care of."

"You think of everything," she said, though her tone wasn't entirely complimentary.

Ignoring the jibe, he winked at her. "Six o'clock," he reminded her and headed for the door. He stopped briefly to whisper something to Peg, who laughed and sneaked a quick look in Kate's direction.

"What the devil were the two of you conspiring about?" Katie asked her aunt.

"We were not conspiring," Peg said, regarding her indignantly. "Luke was just making a comment about the weather. It's gonna be another scorcher today." She fanned herself with a menu as if to emphasize it.

"It's air-conditioned in here," Katie reminded her before walking away in disgust. They were up to something. She knew it.

Even so, she was ready promptly at six. Luke joined her a moment later, wearing the same suit he'd worn for their wedding. Before Katie could catch her breath and comment on how handsome he looked, Ginger bounded down the stairs in a dress Katie had never seen before and slinky high heels. Mrs. Jeffers, wearing a grey silk suit and an abundance of perfume, followed on the arm of Mr. O'Reilly, who was dressed fit to kill, as well.

Obviously she and Luke were not going out for a romantic dinner, Katie decided with some disappointment just as Peg turned up wearing her best dress, the one she usually saved for holidays and weddings.

"Everybody ready?" Luke asked cheerfully.

Katie planted her feet and regarded him warily. "What's this all about? And where is Robby?"

"Robby is with Lucy and Max. Now stop asking so many questions or you'll spoil the surprise."

"I really hate surprises," she muttered.

"Since when?" Peg asked, urging her toward the door. "From the time you were a little, bitty thing, you loved surprises."

"Not anymore," she declared right before her mouth went slack with shock.

Outside, a long, sleek limousine was parked at the curb. Half the neighborhood was standing around gawking at it. Her boarders strolled down the sidewalk as regally as any royalty on earth. Even Ginger managed to act as if this were an everyday occurrence. Katie had no choice but to go along or spoil everyone else's good time, but her suspicious instincts were working overtime.

An hour later as they headed north along the coast, she began to get an inkling of where they were headed at least. There were some wonderful seafood restaurants between Clover and Myrtle Beach. Unfortunately the limo sped past most of them.

Just as she was about to demand answers to all the questions reeling in her head, the limo pulled off the road. Katie peered around at the large, unfamiliar, indistinctive parking lot, then glanced up at the marquee. A smile broke across her face as she read, Appearing Tonight Only, Country Singer Tom Cassidy.

She threw her arms around Luke's neck and kissed him. "You did it! You helped him get a job singing."

Luke shook his head. "As much as I'd like to take the credit, I can't. He did it himself. I just made a couple of calls. The club's owners wouldn't have brought him in if he hadn't performed well at the audition."

"Have you heard him sing?" She thought of the night in her backyard, "I mean really sing, not just fooling around."

"A little at the office one day," he admitted, reminding her of the time she'd called and overheard Tommy's guitar in the background. "It sounded good to me, but I'm tone deaf."

"That's true enough," Katie agreed, but she couldn't seem to stop grinning at him. The fact that he had taken a chance on Tommy, had offered him this shot, it had to mean that the two of them were finally making their peace.

The management of the small restaurant had clearly been expecting them. A special table had been set up near the stage, and they were ushered there with a maximum of fuss. Katie could see that Luke had gone out of his way to see that the others all felt as if they were as special tonight as Tommy. He was as attentive to Mrs. Jeffers as he was to Peg. He teased Ginger and joked with Mr. O'Reilly.

He treated them all like family, Katie thought with a sense of astonishment. A warm feeling of contentment stole through her at the realization.

And when Tommy finally came out to sing, there was no mistaking the pride shining in Luke's eyes. He reached for Katie's hand and clung to it. His foot tapped to the faster rhythms and his eyes shimmered with unshed tears, when Tommy's voice caressed the notes of the more emotional love-gone-wrong songs.

When the mellow tones and words of heartache ended, applause erupted with an enthusiasm that would have rivaled any Garth Brooks concert, albeit the crowd was much smaller. Luke stared around him at the rest of the audience with an unmistakable mix of amazement and delight.

"He was good, wasn't he?" he asked Katie, a grin spreading across his face.

"Fantastic," she confirmed. "Offhand, I'd say your brother has what it takes to make it."

A moment later Tommy emerged from the shadows and walked hesitantly toward them, stopping along the way to accept congratulations from others in the audience. His gaze, though, never left his big brother. When he was only a few feet away, Luke rose and went to meet him.

Katie couldn't hear what was said, but she had no trouble at all guessing what it meant when Luke opened his arms and embraced his brother. Tears clung to her lashes and spilled down her cheeks as she watched them.

Suddenly she felt a slight tug on her arm and turned to look into Ginger's awestruck eyes. "Would you introduce me?" she pleaded. "He is totally awesome!"

Tommy? Awesome? Katie barely hid her grin. Then she took another look at her brother-in-law and realized that she'd been right when she'd told Luke that Tommy's brooding good looks would appeal to women. He'd dressed in black, from his cowboy hat down to his boots. The attire did wicked things to his blue eyes, which seemed brighter and more alive tonight than at any other time Katie could recall.

Katie slid over to the chair Luke had vacated and gestured to Tommy to sit in hers. When she introduced him to Ginger, the teenager's face turned bright red for a second before she gathered her composure. To Katie's astonishment, Tommy seemed equally dumbstruck. She thanked heaven that Ginger's eighteenth birthday was less than a week away. She got the distinct impression that Tommy would be coming to call.

Before she could start worrying about what kind of influence Tommy might be on Ginger or how Luke would feel about him hanging around the boarding house, Luke reached out and tugged her onto the tiny dance floor. His arms came around her and she nestled against his chest.

"Happy?" he asked.

"Very." She looked up at him. "You must be very proud."

"Stunned is more like it. If only I'd listened to him years ago, things might have been different."

"He told you he wanted to sing years ago?"

"Once or twice. I told him it was impractical and dismissed it." He sighed. "I think that was really behind his running off, maybe even more so than Betty Sue's pregnancy. If only I hadn't been so bull-headed, so certain I knew what was right for him, maybe you and I . . ."

Katie reached up and silenced him with a touch. "There's no point in looking back."

"What about forward, Katie?" he asked, searching her face. "Is there a reason to look forward?"

Katie had no ready answer for that. The future seemed so uncertain. "Let's just concentrate on the present," she said, moving even more tightly into his embrace.

"You can't just live for the moment," Luke protested. "You have to plan ahead, be responsible."

"You're backsliding," she teased him gently. "This very moment is the only one we can control and I, for one, don't want to waste it on a silly argument."

She could feel Luke's grin against her cheek.

"You have better things in mind?" he asked with a hopeful note in his voice.

"Much better," she said, looping her arms around his neck so that she could snuggle closer still.

"Ah, yes," Luke murmured with a sigh. "That is definitely much better."

One song ended and another began. They barely noticed.

"Um, Katie, do you suppose we could plan ahead just a little? Say, maybe for an hour or two from now?"

She laughed. "You can dream, Cassidy, but you can't plan."

"Okay, but just so you know, I am having one very erotic dream."

"Me, too, Cassidy. Me, too."

Unfortunately the dream got waylaid. Just about the time they'd gotten everyone settled after the drive back to Clover, there was a tap on the front door. Luke looked as if he'd like to ignore it, but Katie knew that no one would turn up at that late hour unless it was important.

"If you don't answer it, I will," she said.

"Entertaining visitors was not what I had in mind," he said, his gaze roaming over her provocatively one last time just as he opened the door. "Tommy! What are you doing here?"

"I thought we should talk."

"Tonight? Can't it wait until morning? Besides, I thought you'd be up until dawn celebrating."

"The only people I want to celebrate with are here," Tommy said, sounding wistful.

"Well, get in here, then," Katie said. She studied Tommy's somber expression and decided celebrating was actually the last thing on his mind. She stood and headed for the stairs. "Why don't I leave the two of you alone?"

Tommy shook his head. "No, stay, please. This involves you, too." He glanced toward the stairs. "Is Robby here?"

Luke shook his head. "He's spending the night with Lucy and Max."

"Good. Then there's no chance he'll overhear."

Luke tensed at once. "Overhear what? Dammit, Tommy, tonight's not the time to get into a custody discussion."

Tommy faced him squarely. "I think it is."

Katie heard the determination in his voice with a sense of amazement. Tommy had changed since his return to Clover. She could see it. It went beyond the new Western clothes, the neatly trimmed hair, his more mature face. There was a quiet resolve about him that she was forced to admire. She had a feeling that when the time came, the judge's decision wouldn't be an easy one. It would have been far more clear-cut if Tommy had remained the rebellious, irresponsible person who'd first run out on his pregnant lover.

Katie clenched her hands nervously and worried that Luke had seriously underestimated his brother's determination to become a part of Robby's life.

"I know you think I just wanted your money," Tommy began. "You've said it often enough." He met Luke's gaze evenly. "But that was never it. I suppose a part of it was that I wanted to hurt you."

"And you were willing to use Robby to do it," Luke said flatly.

"I wasn't thinking about him, not really," Tommy said. "It was a purely selfish decision. In some sort of twisted way, I think I was jealous of him."

Luke regarded him incredulously. "Jealous? Of a baby?"

Tommy shrugged. "Sounds ridiculous when I say it. But he had you in his life, and he came between you and me. I know I used to mess up, and you bailed me out over and over. Seemed like that was just the nature of our relationship. Then Betty Sue got pregnant and you chose her and the baby over me."

"I chose them *because* of you," Luke said, looking faintly bewildered by Tommy's anger and hurt. "You left me no choice. One of us had to do the right thing."

Tommy's smile was rueful. "You never gave me time to figure that out. Just wham-bang, you took care of it. You sacrificed your feelings for Katie." He shot her an apologetic look. "When I saw that, do you know the kind of guilt I felt? I had to stay away. There was no place for me here knowing how many lives I'd wrecked."

"If you felt so much guilt, then how could you fight me for custody of Robby?" Luke asked, looking shaken by everything Tommy had revealed so far.

"Because I knew in my gut it would send you running back here. I hoped Katie would take you back." He sucked in a deep breath, then admitted, "I owed you and I wanted my brother back."

Luke stood and began to pace. He raked his fingers through his hair, before he finally turned to stare down at his brother. "You were willing to go into court and ask for Robby, to try to take him from me and you thought *that* would get me back?"

"No," Tommy said quietly. "I thought it would get your attention."

"Well, it sure as hell did that!" Luke exploded. "Of all the idiotic, selfish, harebrained schemes." He stopped in front of Tommy. "So now what? Why the hell are you here tonight?"

Tommy flinched at his brother's anger, but his own voice didn't waver. "To tell you that I've withdrawn the suit. Whether you believe it or not, I don't think I could have gone through with it, no matter how things had turned out between us."

He looked from Luke to Katie, then back to his big brother. Katie waited for Luke to speak, but he remained silent.

Finally, looking dejected, Tommy sighed and stood up. "I'll be going now." At the door he paused. Without turning around, he whispered, "I love you, Luke."

And then he was gone.

"Luke?"

"Not now, Katie," he said in a tight tone of dismissal.

Katie felt as if she'd been slapped, rejected. They should have been celebrating the end of the custody battle, but there was so much more at stake. Her heart aching for her husband, Katie headed for the stairs. She paused beside him and put her hand on his cheek. It was damp with tears she doubted he was even aware he'd shed. "Are you coming up?"

"Maybe in a while," he said, his expression bleak.

"I'll be waiting," she promised.

But hours later, when sunlight began to spill through the curtains, Katie was still wide-awake and alone. And when she left the house to go to work at the diner, there was no sign of Luke at all.

It was hours before Katie finally saw Luke again. He wandered into the diner right after noon and took a booth in the back. Katie was waiting on customers at the counter. Ginger was waiting on the tables. She came back to Katie within seconds of taking Luke's order.

"He wants to see you."

"Now?" she asked incredulously. She was still too miffed about his running out on her to risk speaking to him in a crowded diner.

"He seems really upset about something," Ginger observed worriedly. "We could switch for a while and you could take the tables. I think everybody has their order right now, anyway. You'd have a few minutes to talk."

Katie shook her head. "This isn't the place," she insisted stubbornly. She didn't want to hear that Luke intended to end their marriage in the middle of the diner. What else could he possibly be so anxious to say that would put that grim expression on his face? "But if you wouldn't mind watching the counter for a few minutes, I could use a break."

"Sure, but..."

"Thanks," she said and ducked into the ladies' room, the one place she was certain Luke wouldn't follow her.

She was still hiding out in the restroom fifteen minutes later, when the door opened and Lucy appeared. "You okay?"

Katie managed a wobbly smile for her best friend. "I've been better. Where'd you come from?"

"I stopped by to see how things were going. Luke told me you were in here. I think he was just about ready to come busting in himself." She studied Katie from head to toe. "So how are you really?"

"I'm scared, Lucy."

"Of losing Robby?"

"Of losing both of them. Tommy's withdrawn his suit. But with the custody issue resolved Luke has no reason to stay married to me."

"Hogwash! He's in love with you. He has been forever."

Katie didn't believe her, but she clung to Lucy's reassurances, anyway. It gave her the strength to emerge from the restroom and face Luke with the whole damn town looking on. There was an odd air of expectancy in the diner, as if everyone knew something was up between the two of them.

Katie would have waited until everyone left, but Luke and Ginger, with a little help from Peg, conspired to force her hand. Ginger had taken over the counter. Peg was handling the tables. They'd left her with only the one station to cover, Luke's booth. Maybe she should have just made a dash for it, but she finally resigned herself to hearing the bad news now and getting it over with.

She marched over to her husband.

"Have a seat," he invited.

"I don't think so. Are you planning to file for divorce now that you have what you want?" she demanded, hands on hips, her chin thrust forward combatively.

Luke seemed taken aback at first. Then his expression turned even more bleak. "I suppose that could be one interpretation of our deal. It wasn't in writing, though."

"Just implied," she agreed.

She drew in a deep breath and decided to go for broke. He might leave, anyway, but he wouldn't go without getting a fight. "Then there was your side of the bargain. I took a look at the books. They're a shambles. Now that everyone is getting ice cream and cookies in the evening, now that the rent has been lowered..." She shrugged. "Looks to me like you have a long way to go to get things straightened out around here."

A faint spark of hope lit his eyes. "You want me to stay?"

She refused to be the only one making an admission here. "If you want to."

"Do you want me to stay?" he repeated insistently.

Katie sighed and relented. Two stubborn people in one marriage was at least one, if not two, too many. "I've wanted you with me since I was twelve years old. Don't you know yet how much I love you?"

"You love me?"

"Oh, for heaven's sakes," she said impatiently. "Do you think you would ever have gotten across that threshold, if I didn't? It didn't have a blasted thing to do with saving this boarding house. I would have managed somehow."

Luke snagged her wrist and toppled her into his arms. Katie felt a heavy sigh shudder through him.

"When Tommy walked out last night, I should have been shouting with joy, but I couldn't. All I could think about was that it was over with us," he murmured against her cheek. "I don't know what I would have done, if you'd said you wanted a divorce."

Katie touched his shadowed cheek. "Why?"

"Because..."

"Not good enough. Why?" She kept her gaze pinned on his.

"You're my best friend."

She smiled. "Better. Keep going."

Suddenly he was laughing. "Because I love you, Caitlyn Cassidy."

"By golly, I think he's got it," she said.

Suddenly Katie heard Mr. O'Reilly's whoop of glee from the next booth, then Mrs. Jeffers' hushed admonishment about eavesdropping.

"What did they say?" Ginger demanded from clear across the diner.

"He said he loves her," Mr. O'Reilly reported.

"Then they're going to stay married?" Ginger asked.

"Sounds that way to me," he confirmed.

Katie and Luke exchanged a look. "I had no idea they even knew what was going on," she said, just as Henrietta Myers started singing a rousing rendition of "Oh Promise Me" at the top of her lungs.

"I guess she's auditioning in case we decide to try another wedding," Luke said. He caressed Katie's cheek. "What do you say? Will you marry me again? A big, splashy wedding with all the trimmings, maybe even five or six bridesmaids?"

Katie could certainly think of five she would want right by her side in front of the altar at St. John's Church—Abby, Hannah, Emma, Sophie and, of course, Lucy. Joy spread through Katie as she looked him straight in the eye.

"I will," she said, throwing her arms around him. "I will."

As it turned out, no bridesmaids were planned for the ceremony in which Caitlyn and Luke Cassidy were to repeat their wedding vows. Instead, a few days later when Abby, Hannah, Emma, Sophie and Lucy heard about Katie's plans for an all-stops-out, traditional wedding, they promptly agreed with her that it was the perfect opportunity for each of them to renew their own wedding vows. All six couples sat around in the boarding house living room making wedding plans at an impromptu gathering that Lucy had pulled together.

"And we'll throw a shower," Sophie Maguire declared. "Katie never had one."

"A lingerie shower," Emma Flint agreed, shooting a heated look at her husband.

"Only if I can come," Luke interjected.

"All right!" Max Ryder chimed in. "Me, too."

"In your dreams," Lucy said to her husband, effectively dashing his hopeful expression.

"You can forget it, too," Katie told Luke, then leaned down to whisper in his ear.

"I'll bet she's promising a private showing just for him later," Hannah guessed.

"Or maybe she's just offering to take the edge off his disappointment tonight," Ford Maguire suggested, drawing a teasing smack from Sophie, who declared that for a sheriff he had a worrisome one-track mind.

"Ever since I met you," he agreed.

Sophie grinned. "Too bad the baby's not big enough yet. She could be the flower girl." She looked at Luke. "Will Robby be ring bearer?"

"If we can keep him away from the cake long enough," Luke said. "He's become obsessed with food now that he's discovered the difference between homemade and store-bought."

"I just want to know who's going to sing?" Lucy asked. "Are we going to be stuck with Henrietta or can you get Tommy back here from Nashville?"

Katie froze as she waited for Luke's reply. He'd said very little about his brother since the night Tommy came by to tell them he'd dropped the custody suit. The next afternoon they'd heard that Tommy had left for Nashville. She started to step in to cover the awkward silence that had fallen, but Luke gave an almost imperceptible shake of his head.

"I'm not sure if Tommy will be able to make it," he said. "He's just trying to get a new career launched. That takes a lot of time."

"But it's going well," Lucy persisted. "You've talked to him?"

"Yes, we've talked," he said, surprising Katie.

The impromptu party went on for another hour, but when it was over, Katie brought up the subject of Tommy again. "You hadn't mentioned talking to him."

"There was nothing to say," Luke said tightly.

"Oh, Luke . . ."

"Drop it, Katie." He brushed a kiss across her lips. "We have more important things to think about."

"The wedding."

He grinned. "That's too far in the future. I was thinking about right now. Upstairs. You and me."

Katie sighed with pleasure. "Now that is definitely an intriguing notion, Luke Cassidy."

"The best one I've had all day?"

"Certainly the best one you've had since the same time last night," she agreed as she led the way up the stairs.

Epilogue

Katie's wedding gown, which seemed to be endless yards of delicate French lace, was the envy of all the other brides as they waited at the back of St. John's Church for the ceremony to begin.

"If you keep weeping on it, you're going to wilt it," Katie chided her aunt.

"It's just that you look so beautiful," Peg said with a sniff.

"I thought I looked beautiful last time," Katie retorted.

"But this time you really look like a bride." Peg squeezed her hand. "You're happy, aren't you?"

"Happier than I've ever been," Katie said as the first faint sounds of music drifted outside.

Lucy walked over. "Show time, sweetie."

Katie reached out and hugged her. "What would I do without you to feed me my cue at my weddings?"

"Hopefully this will be the very last time I ever have to do it."

"It will be," Katie said with certainty.

The six women lined up in order of their weddings—Abby, Hannah, Emma, Sophie, Lucy and finally Katie. As if she'd never gone through a wedding ceremony before, butterflies swam in Katie's stomach as she watched each of them enter the church and begin the slow walk down the aisle to join their husbands.

At last it was her turn. Robby waited until Katie was at the door before stepping into the aisle, proudly holding the pillow bearing Katie's and Luke's rings.

"Now, Mommy?" he whispered loudly enough to be heard all the way to the front of the church.

Mommy! Katie's heart flipped over. She swooped down and hugged him. "You bet. Let's do it."

Luke's gaze locked on her and never wavered as she made the slow walk down the aisle. Katie thought she would burst with sheer joy as she looked into those dear, familiar blue eyes. She was about to marry the man she loved all over again. She had a son. Her aunt's doubts about her marriage to Luke had finally been put to rest. If only Tommy could be there to share this with them, she thought, then banished the sad thought from her head as she placed her hand in Luke's and waited to repeat her vows with the other couples.

Katie was certain that her voice and Luke's could be heard above all the others, stronger and more certain.

Whether it was true or not hardly mattered, because she cared only about the possessive light shining in her husband's eyes as he declared, "I will love you and honor you, cherish and keep you all the days of our lives."

Forever, Katie thought with a sense of wonder. It was a dream come true. She gazed at the five other equally solemn couples and saw that each pair had eyes only for each other. They had been blessed, all of them.

When the vows had been said and the organ music began to swell, they turned and headed down the aisle. Not until they reached the back of the church did Katie spot Tommy in the shadows, Ginger standing at his side, a challenging glint in her eyes as if she anticipated Luke's disapproval.

Luke spotted his brother at precisely the same moment and for the space of a heartbeat, Katie saw a muscle working in his jaw. Then a sigh shuddered through him and he closed the distance between them.

Katie watched the reunion with her heart in her throat. Then she joined them, just as Robby came racing down the aisle. He skidded to a stop at the sight of Tommy.

"You look like Daddy. Who are you?"

Tommy hunkered down in front of him and held out his hand. "I'm your daddy's brother," he said, looking up at Luke. "That makes me your uncle."

Katie released the breath she hadn't even realized she'd been holding. "Thank you," she mouthed silently to Tommy.

He winked at her. "Some things were just meant to be."

Yes, Katie thought, gazing up at her husband. Some things were just meant to be.

* * * * *

Silhouette®

SPECIAL EDITION™®

COMING NEXT MONTH

Celebration 1000! Begins With:
#991 MAGGIE'S DAD—Diana Palmer
Celebration 1000!
Returning home, Antonia Hayes was determined not to fall again for Powell Long. But the single dad was sexier than ever—and he had *definite* ideas about their reunion!

#992 MORGAN'S SON—Lindsay McKenna
Morgan's Mercenaries: Love and Danger
Rescuing a little boy hit close to home for high-risk expert Sabra Jacobs. Mercenary Craig Talbot knew they faced perilous odds on this mission—but the real danger was losing his heart to her....

#993 CHILD OF MINE—Jennifer Mikels
Ambitious and practical Alex Kane needed one thing: to get his son back. But that meant marrying carefree and outgoing Carly Mitchell, and once they'd said their vows, it was obvious this marriage would *not* be in name only!

#994 THE DADDY QUEST—Celeste Hamilton
Precocious Zane McPherson was on a quest to find a daddy who'd be the perfect match for his mom, Holly. Tough cop Brooks Casey never entertained the idea of being a family man—but one look at Holly had Brooks changing his mind!

#995 LOGAN'S BRIDE—Christine Flynn
The Whitaker Brides/Holiday Elopement
Samantha Gray knew Logan Whitaker was trouble the moment she saw him. She'd only wanted a secure future for her children, but falling for the sexy rancher seemed inevitable—and resisting his tempting offer of marriage was even harder....

#996 BRAVE HEART—Brittany Young
No-nonsense lawyer Rory Milbourne didn't believe in fate. But Daniel Blackhawk knew it was destiny that had brought Rory to him—and that she was the other half of his heart he'd been waiting all his life to find....

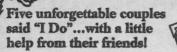

Become a Privileged Woman,
You'll be entitled to all these Free Benefits. And Free Gifts, too.

To thank you for buying our books, we've designed an exclusive FREE program called *PAGES & PRIVILEGES*™. You can enroll with just one Proof of Purchase, and get the kind of luxuries that, until now, you could only read about.

BIG HOTEL DISCOUNTS

A privileged woman stays in the finest hotels. And so can you—at up to 60% off! Imagine standing in a hotel check-in line and watching as the guest in front of you pays $150 for the same room that's only costing you $60. Your *Pages & Privileges* discounts are good at Sheraton, Marriott, Best Western, Hyatt and thousands of other fine hotels all over the U.S., Canada and Europe.

FREE DISCOUNT TRAVEL SERVICE

A privileged woman is always jetting to romantic places.

When <u>you</u> fly, just make one phone call for the lowest published airfare at time of booking— <u>or double the difference back!</u>

PLUS—you'll get a $25 voucher to use the first time you book a flight AND <u>5% cash back on every ticket you buy thereafter through the travel service!</u>